The Case of the Missing Diary

A Chief Inspector Pointer Mystery

By A. E. Fielding

Originally published in 1935

The Case of the Missing Diary

© 2015 Resurrected Press
www.ResurrectedPress.com

Published by Resurrected Press

This classic book was handcrafted by Resurrected Press. Resurrected Press is dedicated to bringing high quality classic books back to the readers who enjoy them. These are not scanned versions of the originals, but, rather, quality checked and edited books meant to be enjoyed!

Please visit ResurrectedPress.com to view our entire catalogue!

For news and updates, visit us on Facebook! Facebook.com/ResurrectedPress

ISBN 13: 978-1-943403-08-0

Printed in the United States of America

Other Resurrected Press books in
The Chief Inspector Pointer <u>*Mystery*</u> Series

RESURRECTED PRESS CLASSIC MYSTERY CATALOGUE

Journeys into Mystery
Travel and Mystery in a More Elegant Time

The Edwardian Detectives
Literary Sleuths of the Edwardian Era

Gems of Mystery
Lost Jewels from a More Elegant Age

Anne Austin
One Drop of Blood
The Black Pigeon
Murder at Bridge

E. C. Bentley
Trent's Last Case: The Woman in Black

Ernest Bramah
Max Carrados Resurrected:
The Detective Stories of Max Carrados

Agatha Christie
The Secret Adversary
The Mysterious Affair at Styles

Octavus Roy Cohen
Midnight

Freeman Wills Croft
The Ponson Case
The Pit Prop Syndicate

J. S. Fletcher
The Herapath Property
The Rayner-Slade Amalgamation
The Chestermarke Instinct
The Paradise Mystery
Dead Men's Money
The Middle of Things
Ravensdene Court
Scarhaven Keep
The Orange-Yellow Diamond
The Middle Temple Murder
The Tallyrand Maxim
The Borough Treasurer
In the Mayor's Parlour
The Saftey Pin

R. Austin Freeman
The Mystery of 31 New Inn from the Dr. Thorndyke
Series
John Thorndyke's Cases from the Dr. Thorndyke
Series
The Red Thumb Mark from The Dr. Thorndyke Series
The Eye of Osiris from The Dr. Thorndyke Series
A Silent Witness from the Dr. John Thorndyke Series
The Cat's Eye from the Dr. John Thorndyke Series
Helen Vardon's Confession: A Dr. John Thorndyke
Story
As a Thief in the Night: A Dr. John Thorndyke Story
Mr. Pottermack's Oversight: A Dr. John Thorndyke
Story
Dr. Thorndyke Intervenes: A Dr. John Thorndyke
Story
The Singing Bone: The Adventures of Dr. Thorndyke
The Stoneware Monkey: A Dr. John Thorndyke Story
The Great Portrait Mystery, and Other Stories: A
Collection of Dr. John Thorndyke and Other Stories
The Penrose Mystery: A Dr. John Thorndyke Story

The Uttermost Farthing: A Savant's Vendetta

Arthur Griffiths
The Passenger From Calais
The Rome Express

Fergus Hume
The Mystery of a Hansom Cab
The Green Mummy
The Silent House
The Secret Passage

Edgar Jepson
The Loudwater Mystery

A. E. W. Mason
At the Villa Rose

A. A. Milne
The Red House Mystery

Baroness Emma Orczy
The Old Man in the Corner

Edgar Allan Poe
The Detective Stories of Edgar Allan Poe

Arthur J. Rees
The Hampstead Mystery
The Shrieking Pit
The Hand In The Dark
The Moon Rock
The Mystery of the Downs

Mary Roberts Rinehart
Sight Unseen and The Confession

Dorothy L. Sayers

Whose Body?

Sir William Magnay
The Hunt Ball Mystery

Mabel and Paul Thorne
The Sheridan Road Mystery

Louis Tracy
The Strange Case of Mortimer Fenley
The Albert Gate Mystery
The Bartlett Mystery
The Postmaster's Daughter
The House of Peril
The Sandling Case: What Would You Have Done?

Charles Edmonds Walk
The Paternoster Ruby

John R. Watson
The Mystery of the Downs
The Hampstead Mystery

Edgar Wallace
The Daffodil Mystery
The Crimson Circle

Carolyn Wells
Vicky Van
The Man Who Fell Through the Earth
In the Onyx Lobby
Raspberry Jam
The Clue
The Room with the Tassels
The Vanishing of Betty Varian
The Mystery Girl
The White Alley
The Curved Blades

FOREWORD

The period between the First and Second World Wars has rightly been called the "Golden Age of British Mysteries." It was during this period that Agatha Christie, Dorothy L. Sayers, and Margery Allingham first turned their pens to crime. On the male side, the era saw such writers as Anthony Berkeley, John Dickson Carr, and Freeman Wills Crofts join the ranks of writers of detective fiction. The genre was immensely popular at the time on both sides of the Atlantic, and by the end of the 1930's one out of every four novels published in Britain was a mystery.

While Agatha Christie and a few of her peers have remained popular and in print to this day, the same cannot be said of all the authors of this period. With so many mysteries published in the period, it is inevitable that many of them would become obscure or worse, forgotten, often with no justification other than changing public tastes. The case of Archibald Fielding is one such, an author, who though popular enough to have a career spanning two decades and more than two dozen mysteries, has become such a cipher that his, or as seems more likely, her real identity has become as much a mystery as the books themselves.

While the identity of the author may forever remain an unsolved puzzle, there are some facts that may be inferred from the texts. It is likely that the author had an upbringing and education typical of the British upper middle class in the period before the Great War with all that implies; a familiarity with the classics, the arts, and music, a working knowledge of modern European languages, an appreciation of the finer things in life. The author certainly had also traveled abroad, primarily in the south of France, but probably to Belgium, Spain, and Italy as well, as portions of several of the books are set in those locales.

The books attributed to Archibald Fielding, A. E. Fielding, or Archibald E. Fielding, are quintessential Golden Age British mysteries. They include all the attributes, the country houses, the tangled webs of relationships, the somewhat feckless cast of characters who seem to have nothing better to do with themselves than to murder or be murdered. Their focus is on a middle class and upper class struggling to find themselves in the new realities of the post war era while still trying to live the lifestyle of the Edwardian era. Things are never as they seem, red herrings are distributed liberally throughout the pages as are the clues that will ultimately lead to the solution of "the puzzle," for the British mysteries of this period are centered on the puzzle element which both the reader and the detective must solve before the last page.

A majority of the Fielding mysteries involve the character of Chief Inspector Pointer. Unlike the eccentric Belgian Hercule Poirot, the flamboyant Lord Peter Wimsey, or the somewhat mysterious Albert Campion, Pointer is merely a competent, sometimes clever, occasionally intuitive policeman. And unlike, as with Inspector French in the stories of Freeman Wills Croft, the emphasis is on the mystery itself, not the process of detection.

Pointer is nearly as much of a mystery as the author. Very little of his personal life is revealed in the books. He is described as being vaguely of Scottish ancestry whose father was a Coast guardsman on the Devon coast.. He is well read and educated, though his duties at Scotland Yard prevent him from enjoying those pursuits. In an early book in the series it is revealed that he spends a week or two each year climbing mountains, his only apparent recreation, though before becoming a policeman he'd played football for the All England team. His success as a detective depends on his willingness to "suspect everyone" and to not being tied to any one theory. He is fluent in French, German, and Italian and familiar with those countries. He is, at least in the first two books, unmarried, and sharing lodgings with a bookbinder named O'Connor, in much the manner of Holmes and Watson, though this character is absent in the later works. *The Case of the Missing Diary* adds little to our knowledge of Pointer, as from his first appearance in Chapter Three he is too caught up in the case for personal matters to intrude.One intriguing feature of the Pointer mysteries is that they all involve an unexpected twist at the end, wherein the mystery finally solved is often not the mystery invoked at the beginning of the book. *The Case of the Missing Diary* is no exception. Fielding introduces numerous red-herrings and subplots to confuse the reader while still largely playing fair with the reader. When Fielding wrote *The Case of the Missing Diary* the series was already ten years old, the book being the seventeenth novel to feature Chief Inspector Pointer. The author's style had matured and been refined over that period. Gone are the over reliance on disguises and other dramatic gimmicks that mark some of the earlier books. There is much more reliance on solid detection, the interpretation of clues, and judging the validity of the testimony of those involved. Yet, the Pointer mysteries have a certain flair that separates them from the "humdrum" school of mysteries that were starting to appear at the same time. Stylistically, they fall somewhere between the works of Christie and those of Ngaio Marsh or E. C. R. Lorac.

The Case of the Missing Diary involves the murder of Charles Dawnay, whose body is discovered in the summer-house which he uses as a study and retreat. At first, it is supposed that the culprit is a local character named Gypsy Joe who had been at odds with Dawnay over the accidental killing of a dog, but Pointer soon becomes dissatisfied with this solution. Several possible motives for various parties come to light, involving an inheritance, business dealings, and romances actual or intended. As it becomes crucial to determine who had appointments with the victim in the hours leading up to the murder, it is hoped that Dawnay's diary, in which he kept meticulous notes fo such matters, will provide vital clues, but this hope is dashed when the diary proves to be written in an indecipherable code, and, may not, in fact, actually be Dawnay's diary at all.

In typical Fielding fashion, *The Case of the Missing Diary* confuses the reader with false clues and irrelevant plot lines that prove to be dead ends. Complicating Pointer's task is the fact that each of the suspects seems to have something which they are hiding and conflicts with the other characters. This leaves the inspector, and the reader, to determine which one is guilty of the murder, and which ones are only guilty of some other crime.

Despite their obscurity, the mysteries of Archibald Fielding, whoever he or she might have been, are well written, well crafted examples of the form, worthy of the interest of the fans of the genre. It is with pleasure, then, that Resurrected Press presents this new edition of *The Case of the Missing Diary* and other books in the series to its readers.

About the Author

The identity of the author is as much a mystery as the plots of the novels. Two dozen novels were published from 1924 to 1944 as by Archibald Fielding, A. E. Fielding, or Archibald E. Fielding, yet the only clue as to the real author is a comment by the American publishers, H.C. Kinsey Co. that A. E. Fielding was in reality a "middle-aged English woman by the name of Dorothy Feilding whose peacetime address is Sheffield Terrace, Kensington, London, and who enjoys gardening."

Research on the part of John Herrington has uncovered a person by that name living at 2 Sheffield Terrace from 1932-1936. She appears to have moved to Islington in 1937 after which she disappears. To complicate things, some have attributed the authorship to Lady Dorothy Mary Evelyn Moore nee Feilding (1889-1935), however, a grandson of Lady Dorothy denied any family knowledge of such authorship. The archivist at Collins, the British publisher, reports that any records of A. Fielding were presumably lost during WWII. Birthdates have been given variously as 1884, 1889, and 1900. Unless new information comes to light, it would appear that the real authorship must remain a mystery.

Greg Fowlkes
Editor-In-Chief
Resurrected Press
www.ResurrectedPress.com
www.Facebook.com/ResurrectedPress

CHAPTER ONE

CHARLES DAWNAY stopped close by the Bank of England to buy some matches from an old soldier who, with his one remaining hand, drew quite pretty little silhouettes of the Old Lady of Threadneedle Street on his boxes. Another man was just turning away as Dawnay stepped up, and something about him was vaguely familiar. He turned and caught Dawnay's eye, and on his face too was the same look of half-recognition. Then he smiled.

"Mr. Charles Dawnay, I think?" he said interrogatively. "We spent a week together two years ago—"

"Cricket week at Colonel Harper's," Dawnay supplemented. He had placed the other now. "And you did some prodigious batting." They shook hands. The name came back to Dawnay as he did so. Mallinson . . . a young solicitor with sound views on body line bowling and an interest in company promoting. They walked on together, chatting.

After a moment or two Mallinson held out his hand again. His road now branched off to the left.

"By the way," he said idly, "I think I know a cousin of yours—name of Walter Lyall—I see quite a good deal of him."

Dawnay's eyes, large and bright behind their glasses, turned to him swiftly. "I hope to heaven you haven't anything to do with my Cousin Walter in the way of business," he said fervently.

Mallinson looked at him.

"Why not? I'm buying a proposition of his. A very good bit of business."

"Couldn't be. Not if it's Walter's," was the decided reply.

"I've had it investigated. It looks thoroughly sound." Mallinson's tone was that of a man not easily shaken from his own opinion by that of other men.

"It would," retorted Dawnay cheerfully, "but it won't be ones. Better have a talk with me before you close the deal, if it's anything to do with one of his Bolivian or Peruvian ventures."

It was, as a matter of fact, connected with Bolivia, but Mallinson showed no sign of anxiety. He was generally called "poker-face" because of his imperturbability. In figure he was tall and athletic-looking, with a swinging stride of a walk.

"My option's up by noon to-morrow," he said.

"I live at St John's Wood—Regency Avenue," said Dawnay. "I can spare a few minutes this afternoon around four if you're anywhere near there, and would care to drop in." He handed Mallinson his card.

"Glad to," came the reply, as Mallinson put it carefully away. "Thanks very much indeed. Four o'clock then. It's very good of you."

Just then another man hurried up level with them and touched Dawnay on the arm.

"I've been trying to catch up. Come back with me in my car. I want you to see some fresh papers that have just arrived."

"Sorry." Dawnay's tone was cool as he drew away. "I haven't a moment to spare to-day. To-morrow will be time enough. At four then!" he said to Mallinson.

"At four!" Mallinson echoed the two words and hurried away.

He had a couple of appointments which he could not put off, but he raced through them, in order to go again, very carefully, through all the papers relating to the deal with Walter Lyall. They seemed satisfactory. The ore was not first-class, but it contained wolfram as well as gold, and the property seemed well worth the price asked for it. The geological report was most promising. Finally he locked the papers away. He could see no holes in the proposition, but he looked thoughtful. He had already had to mortgage himself up to the hilt to be able to pay the option money the next day.

Dawnay had walked on after his parting with Mallinson, deep in thought. Walter again! Walter with his absolute untrustworthiness. So far, he had not—apparently—over-stepped the line which separates the proven from the suspected criminal; but one day he would, of that Dawnay was certain. If only he could be got out of the country. Dawnay had long wanted to come on some piece of work of Walter's which would justify his delivering an ultimatum—Walter's departure for some distant country and his residence there, in return for silence and no prosecution. It sounded rather like blackmail, Dawnay admitted to himself ruefully, but it was the only way by which Walter could be eliminated. And lately he had had the colossal impudence to pay marked attention to Clare, Dawnay's much younger sister.

Dawnay recalled his wandering thoughts. He would have a talk with Walter now, if he could find him in his office—for Walter called himself a mining engineer too—and arrange for him to drop in at five at St. John's Wood, after Mallinson had been—after he, Dawnay, knew just what it was that Walter hoped to sell the solicitor. Mallinson seemed a clever enough chap, and Walter would have seen to it that there was nothing wrong on the surface with his proposal, but something told Dawnay that at last he might be able to send Walter off for years; long enough for Clare to be married and forget he ever existed; long enough to prevent his using his relationship with himself, Dawnay, as he had in the past.

Dawnay glanced at his watch and stepped in at his bank. After which he found Walter and had a brief but very guarded word with him—Walter must not be frightened away before Dawnay knew what his proposition was—and then hurried to Liverpool Street Station to see Edie and their two little girls off for

Cromer. He was a few minutes late, and Edith was standing looking out for him, watching the clock, her face upturned. It was not an easy-going face. Here was a woman, one would say, quick to notice slights and to resent them, perhaps even to fancy them. But with her youth and looks, slights had, so far, not come her way. Her father had given Charles a word of warning at their wedding. "Love her, Charles, and show her that you love her." Then the champagne had made him add under his breath, "If you don't, there'll be the devil to pay! And Charles had always shown her that he loved her.

Certainly his face did so now, as he hurried towards her; and hers, haughty, imperious and dark, had melted into instant tenderness at sight of him.

There was passion in the way she returned his kiss, regardless of others on the platform or of the nurses with the children.

"To think I'm going away for another whole fortnight," she said in a half whisper. "Oh, Charlie, how shall I stand it!"

He murmured something similar.

"Don't fall in love with any one while I'm away," she said, getting into a compartment and setting her hat still farther over one eye, "there aren't many wives who would leave you with a handsome young housekeeper for weeks on end as I've done."

"Ah, Miss Miller is a danger," he agreed mockingly, "that is to say to any elderly, plain wife like yourself." He got no further and they both burst out laughing.

"She's going to have the house smartened up beyond all recognition by the time you get back with the infants," he continued after a moment. The two little girls, their only children, had fallen ill with scarlet fever while staying with their grandmother in the country. Edith had rushed to them, for things had looked very black, leaving the house in St. John's Wood in charge of a very competent young woman, a distant relation of Charles', who was going in for a Domestic Science course at King's

College. For three weeks Edith had only been able to rush up to town for an hour or so at intervals, and now, she and the children and the nurses were off to the seaside.

"That reminds me. She told me this morning to give you a message about your grey carpet." He felt in his pocket for a diary notebook which he always carried. She watched him with a fond smile.

"You and your entries! If you ever commit a murder, Charlie, the police will find it fully jotted down., with memos such as,'Remember to account for the above hour,' 'Send coat to the cleaners with a word about removing bloodstains—'"

"I always jot things down at once," he agreed. "An engineer has to remember too many figures for him to trust to his unaided memory, however good. Here it is—" He read out: "Tell Edie the cleaners say the carpet will look like new if the more expensive process is used. Edie to say if she wants it done." He looked at her interrogatively, pencil in hand. She considered.

"I think it'll be too dear for such an old thing," she decided. "Especially as I doubt their promises. Cleaners will promise anything, in my experience."

He jotted the word "no" beside the entry, and put the book away. "Cynic!" he said as he did so.

The word seemed to strike her. She stood a moment as though debating whether to speak or keep silent, then she turned to him slowly. As a rule, Edie was quick as a bird in her movements.

"I'm anything but a cynic," and she spoke slowly now, "but I think one shouldn't be gulled, Charlie. I don't call it being suspicious to notice things—" She looked at him fixedly, and he had a feeling as though she were weighing her next words, which was surely an absurd idea.

"Nor do I!" he assented cheerily. "I'm considered quite nippy in that line myself. Have to be. But what have you noticed in especial?" For he was certain that she was preparing the way for some point, some topic, about which she wanted to speak to him.

He had a feeling that she was hesitating afresh now, before she replied:

"I'm thinking about Sebastian."

He stared. Why all the preamble, he wondered.

He knew that Edie didn't like Sebastian. This long absent cousin of his had turned up just before her dash to her children's bedside. Charles had at once insisted on putting him up for a fortnight, but the fortnight had run on to three weeks and would probably continue until Edith came back from Cromer. Sebastian and he got on splendidly. The very fact that it was twenty years since the former had left England, just the year Charles went to Cambridge, made it all the easier, perhaps. They met as strangers and yet with ties in common. Edie had seemed to share his feeling at first, but gradually something cold, distant, almost inimical had crept into her manner, showing more clearly on each of her swift visits to the house.

"And I know what you're thinking about the poor chap," he said now, feelingly. "I assure you, darling, that he wasn't drunk last Sunday. He was only playing at lost memory—"

She gave him a steady look. "I don't think he was drunk either," she said gravely, "but I don't think he was playing at lost memory, either. I don't think he had an idea what you were referring to."

"You think he'd really forgotten old Sampson! Impossible!" he said with certainty. "One forgets useful things, but never your old nannie's name, or idiotic family jokes."

"I quite agree with you," she said. "And don't you see that I also agree with what that means?" Charles Dawnay was keen-witted, but here he was baffled.

"No, I don't," he said bluntly.

"What steps did you take to be sure that the man really is Sebastian?" she said finally. "There, it's out! Though I hadn't meant to speak of it, but write of it to you. I think he's been taken much too much for granted.

He just rang the bell and told us he was Sebastian and we both fell on his neck and welcomed him back to the old country and took him down with us to Trenders for a week."

"Yes, and he knew every stick and stone and hedge and field down there," Charles said instantly.

"He seemed to know it all very well," she agreed, "but still—" she stopped. "I'm not at all sure that he wasn't just recognising things from descriptions given him—or from what he had read," she said meaningly.

"Look here," he said urgently, "what have you got to go on? What suggested such an amazing idea?"

"A lot of little things," she said at once. "You told me yourself that he was changed out of all knowledge. I have only seen him once before."

"Of course, he's changed enormously," Charles said thoughtfully, "but he looks very much as Sebastian would be expected to look after twenty years of sun—"

"And spirits," she finished. Sebastjan's reputation in the family did not glitter. "But the first time I ran in after you got back from Trenders, I found him deep in those old photographic albums on the top shelf—the Family Vaults as you call them—poring over snapshots of Sebastian."

"Of himself? Why not? Oneself as a kid is a stranger, and rather a pathetic stranger, too."

"Oh, quite so. But you don't surround yourself with photographs of those years and stare at them as though memorising them. But it wasn't that only. It's lots of things. For instance, he looked all at sea when you talked about the dog who used to curl up with the cat—"

"Memory isn't his long suit, evidently."

"But he pretends it is," she added quietly. "I talked with him on last Monday, when I dashed up for half an hour and you weren't back. We talked a lot about you and the rest of the family as boys. Well, he was shy of two of you."

"Which two?" Charles asked with curiosity.

"Of Lawrence Dawnay and of yourself. Now I know that Sebastian went out to Africa years and years ago to join your cousin Lawrence, didn't he?"

"Yes. They stayed together for nearly a year. Longest time poor old Sebastian ever stuck to any job."

"Just so. Yet he won't venture on any recollections of Lawrence, nor of that time. No more than he cares to be precise about you. Yet when I told him a lot of reminiscences which I had heard from you about your summer together on the Broads, he fell into the trap."

"You told him—my dear girl, what a little swindler you are!"

"You set traps to catch mice, and rats, and things you don't want about the house, don't you?" she flashed back. "But about your reminiscences of the Broads—as re-told by me, he remembered them all. Or nearly all! And embroidered one or two quite nicely!"

And at that, Charles did look uneasy. "But why should any one want to impersonate poor old Sebastian?" he said as though trying to reassure himself. "He never had a bean. This Sebastian's quite well off, if not wealthy. He's asked me about some good investments for a sum of thirty thousand, and didn't speak as though that were all his wealth by any means—"

"And you didn't ask him how he got it?" she asked.

"I did. He told me he'd done well in the South African Markets buying gold shares when they were worth as many pence as they are pounds to-day, and then by out-and-out gambling on them. He spoke of quite a pile besides the thirty thousand."

"He wants you to invest the thirty thousand for him?" she queried swiftly, suspicion in her eye.

He nodded. "Perhaps. Advise him anyway."

There was a silence. "I don't see how he can be an impostor," he said finally. "He knows too much about us all, and the old house. Besides—oh, no, Edie, it's impossible! He's got the Dawnay face and voice. No, no, I feel sure he's all right."

"You hadn't heard from Sebastian for some time, had you?"

"Two years and more," he replied.

"How does he explain them?" she asked.

"Says he was too busy with the Stock Markets to think of letters. I was relieved, for more than once—" he hesitated.

"Yes?" she asked him.

"I had a suspicion from something a chap let drop who didn't know he was a relative, that Sebastian might have got himself into serious trouble with the I.D.B. men. He was in Namaqualand when the first stones were found, I knew. . ."

Again there was a silence.

"Frankly, I had an idea he might even be in prison—under another name," Charles said finally under his breath. "That's what made me doubly glad to see him safe and sound back in England."

"Didn't Sebastian have a chum with him these last years who looked very like him?" she asked suddenly. "I seem to remember his writing to you about him."

Charles nodded. "Yes, name rather like our own. Dawes, was it? No, Dawson, that was it! Captain Dawson. Lucky for Sebastian he was on hand when he went down with fever. He'd have died, he wrote, but for his friend's care. For 'fever' possibly read D.T., but the result would have been the same."

"And since that time Sebastian's never written you a letter," she said slowly, "only now and then a picture postcard . . . and they stopped last year. . ."

"I'll look into it," he said, "though as Sebastian was a penniless wastrel—"

"I liked him," she said to that. "Do you remember that dance when you were going up to Cambridge and he was off for South Africa—the dance at which you and I met, I met him too that night, and he made quite an impression?"

She gave the smile with which a woman recalls a long vanished bit of romance. "He seemed so dashing and such a pioneer!" She gave Charles' arm a squeeze. "I don't mind confessing—now—that that is really what first made me suspect this Sebastian He had forgotten that dance! Forgotten the rose I gave him! Forgotten that we had kissed-good-bye. Yes, we did!" She laughed up at her husband. "You were only eighteen then," she said with dancing eyes," and I was sixteen and Sebastian was a man of the world! Heavens, how he impressed me!"

"He was only four years older than me." Charles said, rather crossly.

"Ah, but he was down from Oxford, you only just going up to Cambridge. He was off on the Grand Tour! Anyway, it lasted for nearly the whole week, did the memory of that little episode. He wrote me once—afterwards and I couldn't quite place him!" And she gave a little laugh. "So much for a young girl's dream. But do you think Sebastian could forget me so utterly? Am I vain to doubt it?"

Edith had been an enchantingly pretty girl. Charles had fallen in love with her that night, and he for one, had not forgotten one moment of the dance.

"Tell you what, Edie," he said now after a second's reflection, "I'll put a poser to him to-night. Or rather, more than one." He got out his notebook and with a sardonic grin and a jut forward of his strong and masterful jaw wrote in silence for a minute. Then he put the book away with a nod.

"That'll test him! If he can answer those two questions he's Sebastian all right. I'll ask him when we have our before-dinner sherry to-night We're having a quiet bachelor dinner at home—or rather, at the house, not much 'home' about it till you get back."

She gave his arm a swift squeeze.

"I've told Morley to keep an unobtrusive eye on him," she murmured.

Morley was her own maid who was just now acting as the parlourmaid. She had come with Edith from her mother's house.

"That woman," he said shortly. "Edie, I wish you'd send her away when you get back. She's been most infernally rude to Miss Miller lately. The girl's a sport, and hasn't complained, but I overheard Morley myself."

A curious look flitted over his wife's face; just flitted and was gone.

"Let's go and see how the bambini are getting on," she suggested, and the two forgot for the moment everything else. But when the last moment came, and Charles whispered to his wife how terribly he would miss her and count the hours till she should be back again, she flashed an odd look at him from under her thick lashes. He did not quite like that look. It was probing and it was— distrustful was a ludicrous word to apply to any glance of Edie's at him, but it belonged in that county all the same. But in her smile at him as the train steamed off, in the children's excited calls, he forgot it, and it was a very proud, happy husband and father who stood waving to his family from the platform. Then they passed out of sight, and it was a deeply thoughtful man who stood for a moment alone on the platform reflecting on what he had just learnt. But the more he thought it over, the more certain he felt that Edie was wrong, and that Sebastian would prove to be the genuine article. Those two questions, however, which he had jotted down, would definitely settle the matter, and he patted his pocket almost unconsciously.

Yet as he made for the exit it was Walter who was uppermost in his mind, the hope that at last his kinsman would have delivered himself into his hand.

Walter, as it happened, was lunching with Mallinson at one o'clock. He was ugly and freckled, with an air of bluff honesty which seemed to go with his snub nose.

Even his voice suggested the cricket field, and all that is supposed to go therewith.

Throughout the meal they chatted of unimportant things. As coffee was served, Mallinson remarked that he had happened to run into Charles Dawnay that morning. "You're a cousin of his, I think you said."

Walter made an assenting noise. He shot the other rather a startled glance from his honest blue eyes.

"I had a word with him too," he said hurriedly, "at my office. He was full of some accident he'd just seen. One chap hurrying along bumped into another chap and all but sent him under a bus. He just missed being killed." Walter gave an unfeeling laugh which suggested regret that nothing so exciting had eventuated.

"About that Bolivian concession," Mallinson said next, apparently out of the blue. And there followed a few brief, but very searching questions.

Lyall threw himself into the answers with gusto and his frankest manner.

Mallinson drummed on the table. "So you assure me again that there's no catch anywhere? Nothing I don't know of which would make a difference in my being willing to buy?" he asked finally.

Lyall drew himself up. Like his Cousin Charles, he was, a big, brawny young man.

"My dear Mallinson, do you for an instant think that I would let you down?" His tone was magnificent, and his pose. "Why these questions?" he went on, and he shot the other a stealthy look.

"Your cousin Dawnay." Mallinson lit a cigarette. "I'm seeing him this afternoon, and thought it just as well to go over some of the points again, and be certain that there's no possible hitch anywhere. Certainly I couldn't find any, and I consider myself a fair judge," he added with a pleasant smile.

"My dear Mallinson," Walter Lyall inflated his chest again, "you're on a winner! I wouldn't part with that Concession for double what you're paying, if I didn't happen to be in need of some ready money. It's a gold mine! There are millions in it. Trouble with Charles is, he can't bear to let others have a look in too. What he will try to do will be to crab it—before he grabs it. Ha-ha!" Walter's hearty laugh rang out. "Don't you let him do it! I would much rather sell to you than to him. By the way, what time are you going to see him?"

"Oh, latish. . . Six," Mallinson replied promptly. He had no intention of Lyall dropping in, to join the talk about his proposition.

CHAPTER TWO

"Now what does Lady Ann reply to Julian?" pondered Harry Eliot aloud as he clutched his typewriter's bar and set his teeth.

He must be witty, he must be topical. For Eliot was a writer of film scenarios, a very successful writer indeed; and you didn't come to the front rank in that work without hard labour. He wrote a reply, looked at it, shouted "Tripe!" whacked it out with a row of dashes; wrote another sentence, looked at it, shouted "Synthetic tripe!" and slammed it out with a row of Xs through it. Then he sat back and ran a hand through his thick hair. He needed a change. Life in the country, in a cottage, was the life of a cabbage, he told himself. And as for the joys of gardening—he glared out of his window—latticed-paned of course—at a bed of calceolarias, Paul Crampel geraniums, and blue lobelias. He shut his eyes. A vision of honeysuckle and pinks, lavender hedges, roses, and nodding violas rose before him—the vision he had had when taking the cottage. "Well-stocked garden" had been in the lease. Stocked with wire-worms and slugs had been his experience. And, being a town bird, he had waited too long to see what those fascinating green clumps and wisps were going to turn into. Chiefly nettles and duckweed, he found. A hasty order to a gardener had resulted in a display which would have shamed the most Victorian of front beds. "My God, it only needs standard fuchsias to complete the picture," moaned Eliot, a hand to his brow. He must get away; go somewhere where there was life, minds stirring about him. He had refused Blenkinsop's offer of yachting with him. A life on the ocean wave with Blenkinsop was apt to be strenuous but exciting. It would have done him good, shaken him up. Pity he had turned him down.

His telephone rang. "Charles Dawnay speaking," came a voice.

Eliot brightened. He liked the Dawnays. He had rather thought of dropping in to see Charles Dawnay this week, for he had heard that Sebastian Dawnay was back.

Sebastian had been at Harrow, as had Eliot, though not in the same House. He remembered Sebastian vaguely, but with a reminiscent grin. A lanky, raw hare-brained young daredevil.

"How's your—work getting on?" Dawnay's voice went on. "I saw *The Land Mermaid* the other day, and thought it jolly good."

"I'm stuck," came Eliot's dismal reply, "in the mud in the country, among the cabbages. And sick of them."

"Oh? Then come up and try the King's. My wife's away just now at Cromer with the kids. The kids have lately gone in for scarlet fever on the grand scale. They're recuperating now, but they won't be home for a fortnight. Suppose you come up and stay with me for a bit? Until you get fed up. A pal of mine is staying with me, and my Cousin Sebastian, who is back in England, is staying here too. You were at Harrow with him, weren't you? Know each other? You remember him?"

"Perfectly!" This was a polite exaggeration on Eliot's part.

"Good! Capital!" Dawnay's voice sounded pleased. "Drop in at once then. He's not often in for lunch, but he will be to-day. You can do it easily if you pack quickly, and we'll plan a really amusing afternoon."

Eliot assured Dawnay, after another blink at the calceolarias and Paul Crampels and lobelias, that he could bear to miss the country for a while. Flung sufficient clothes into a suitcase to last for a few days in town; told the only servant he kept that he would phone him his instructions later, and dashed off. He'd like to see what Sebastian had turned into. Something decorous and very conventional probably, since he had run away from home to be a cowboy one summer vacation. He hummed that grand old song, *Forty Years On.* It wasn't quite that, but it was a good twenty.

Dawnay telephoned to Robina Miller to say that he would be lunching at home. She stood by the telephone, a slender, very well-groomed young woman, with a clear bright complexion that went well with her glossy hair and neatly drawn eyebrows. There was pride in the carriage of her small head. Quite unlike Edith Dawnay in any other way, yet there was a resemblance in one respect; she too looked as if she would not meet opposition with meekness. Her pretty nose had a high bridge to it.

"I wish you would go away and let me get on with my shopping lists," she was saying now to Sebastian Dawnay. He eyed her with a grin and did not move. He looked emphatically what is known as "hard-boiled," with his light eyes that stared boldly out of a sunburnt face, hooked nose, and wide, thin-lipped mouth. It was a hard and dissipated, reckless face, and yet a face with a great deal of personal magnetism behind it. He had a magnificent physique, of which he was consciously and unconsciously proud. By the family records, Sebastian was about forty-two. He looked at once older and younger—older in experience, and younger in a sense of enjoying life, of being full of almost overwhelming energies, of being crammed to bursting point with vitality.

"Nonsense, darling," he said, edging closer. She laid a hand on the instrument as though it were a shield.

"I'm about to telephone to Leslie." She spoke as though in warning.

"Boy or girl?" he asked lazily.

"Leslie is the man whom I'm going to marry," she replied hotly.

"And you throw him in my teeth like this!" mocked Sebastian, showing them—rather ugly teeth, broken here and there, and discoloured, but strong as a horse's.

"I told you I was engaged that first time we met."

"When I kissed you. I know," he said and his smile widened.

She flashed a cautious glance over her shoulder, then something about her face suggested that it angered her to have shown that much care for what the servants might hear. "I think you're one of the greatest brutes unhung," she snapped in a genuine temper.

"So you really are going to be married," he went on, leaning comfortably against an open door, hands in pockets, light, bold eyes on her face "I thought Charles was the reason you were so cold to me."

"Quite like Morley," she said with a sneer that it cost her an effort to make, "Mrs. Dawnay's maid I mean. She too seems to think that I'm using Mrs. Dawnay's absence from the house as a heaven-sent chance to ensnare her husband. I had hardly been in the house an hour before she let me see that she suspected me of designs on him If it weren't for the trouble Mrs. Dawnay has been in, the anxiety about the children, I'd leave here—I'd have left the first time that woman spoke to me."

There was no mistaking the passionate resentment in her voice. But Sebastian continued to grin as though he found her very funny.

"I'm hanging on till she comes back, just because I like her," Robina went on, "and know she trusts me. But as for that woman—" She bit her lip.

"You've never forgiven her, and never will," he finished for her. "Nasty temper you've got, Robina. You bear malice, you know. Shouldn't. I never do. Life's too short. You haven't forgiven me yet for that one kiss. Why, my dear child, you might kiss me twenty times, and I wouldn't hold it against you!"

She flung away from him and returned to the telephone, which was ringing.

"Doctor Ozier?" she repeated questioningly, "I don't know. Hold the line, will you." Then she caught sight of the butler. "Weatherall, is Doctor Ozier in his rooms? He is? Will you put this call through to him then," and Robina, picking up her shopping list, walked away.

"Shall I drive you?" Sebastian asked. "I've a new car I'm trying out."

"Thank you, no," she said fervently. "Your driving needs trying out too. Like the car. Mrs. Dawnay said you won a prize once., It must have been in a gymkhana car race!"

He laughed and sauntered off.

Within the hour, Eliot was slowing up in front of the pleasant, double-fronted white Regency house, with its charming garden backing on to Regent's Park. Eliot had stayed here before and found a house full, but Sebastian and pretty vacuous Clare Dawnay, his host's sister, would be company enough.

A tall bronze-faced man standing by the steps came forward and looked at him keenly. Was it? Surely it was! But how changed?

"Sebastian Dawnay, I think?" Eliot said, holding out his hand

"Eliot!" came the swift reply in what sounded like instant recognition and the two shook hands. No, Sebastian Dawnay hadn't changed into anything very tame and conventional after all, decided Eliot.

Turning, they went in together, and Eliot was conscious of a curious element in the man just beside him—curious because he had never met it before. Something about the man imposed itself on you. His mood. Silence it seemed to be just now. Rarely, thought Eliot, faintly amused and distinctly interested, had two old schoolfellows met after twenty years with so little to say. A masterful man strode beside him if he was not mistaken.

"Are you a cowboy?" he asked over his shoulder with a chuckle.

Sebastian burst into a laugh. "Ha ha! Good memory. No, it didn't last long, the gilt on the cowboy business. . . Still, as I'm an owner of some farms in South Africa I suppose in a way might still call myself a cowman—among other things. By the way, Charles is detained for a moment. A Committee Meeting. He left his apologies and told me to make you at home. What'll you take?"

Eliot named it and was duly taking it. He would use Sebastian for his next act. Lady Ann, carried away by his experienced and adventurous air, is half inclined to fall in love with him, half inclined to marry the curate. In the end she takes neither; but for the adventurer Sebastian should make a good study.

A tall thin girl came in. Very trim, very efficient, very smart she looked, he thought, remembering the pretty woolliness of Clare Dawnay.

"Have you two ever met?" Sebastian asked. He had a clear, hard voice. "Miss Miller—my distant kinswoman—rushed to Charles' assistance when Mrs. Dawnay had to leave him alone. She runs the house. Runs all of us—" he shot the girl a quizzical look. She flushed slightly as she shook hands. Something in her quick brown eyes made Eliot think that she was being badgered by this man. She was interesting and vivid-looking if not exactly pretty, and he would have expected her to be quite able to hold her own. But glancing under cover of a smile at Sebastian Dawnay he sensed again the masterfulness of the man, the something compelling, almost daunting—an absurd word. First-rate study for his next scene anyway.

The three of them sat talking and smoking until Charles Dawnay arrived. Then they strolled in to lunch.

Dawnay himself was a big man, big as Sebastian, and not unlike him in looks, but in a different way.

His eyes were the same colour, but they were merely alert and quick. His face had no such lines ploughed into its tan.

Dawnay was very silent to-day, Eliot thought. And he had an odd sensation of being watched, of Dawnay seeming to stand aside waiting for something, especially when he spoke to Sebastian.

Dr. Ozier, Dawnay's especial friend, a young medical man engaged on research work, was not down, but then no one seemed to expect Ozier to be on time. He would come, Robina said, as soon as something had blown up, or boiled over. It occurred to Eliot that the house must be a bit dull for a young woman. But as Miss Miller was attending classes at King's College in her spare time she probably preferred it so.

"Suppose we lunch in the summer-house?" Dawnay suggested, looking around the dining-room.

The summer-house was his den, and the spot where he spent practically all the daylight hours when at home.

"Morley thought it looked like rain," Robina said dryly. "She practically insisted on our having the meal set in here. She's acting as parlourmaid since Jones left, you know."

Dawnay took his place without another word. It was a handsome white room with windows along one end of it, one of which was a bay window. The bay was curtained off just now with deep green curtains, making an effective splash of colour.

To Eliot there was something odd about the meal that followed. Odd in the sense that Dawnay, usually the most genial of hosts, was by turns jolly, and abruptly silent.

Miss Miller fortunately seemed quite at her ease, and chatted away about the preparations for Mrs. Dawnay's home-coming. She wanted to get some new covers finished before Edith should return. It meant a lot of work for herself in the fortnight remaining, but she seemed very keen on it, speaking of it as a pleasure, and referring to Edith Dawnay with great affection.

Suddenly Dawnay turned to the two men. "You don't seem to have much to say to one another!" he protested, and began talking about Harrow.

Eliot was only too glad to give his tongue a run, and chimed in gaily. Sebastian contented himself with grunts, and nods, and, only when he could not get out of it, with a few words—the fewest possible. He made an odd blunder,

Eliot thought, but when he chaffed him about his memory, Sebastian yawned openly. "My school days lie buried as far, as I am concerned," he said frankly. "Few of us really were happy at school. I wasn't."

And suddenly Eliot remembered that there had been some whispers about his leaving, just whispers, but to the effect that he would not have been taken back in any case. Eliot tried to recall what it was supposed to have been about. Ragging one of the junior masters— something of that sort. Nothing discreditable but not exactly praiseworthy.

Again the talk swung around to some patterns of wallpaper that Robina wanted Charles Dawnay to order. He said he would make a note of it, and put his hand in his pocket for his notebook. Drawing it out, he opened it and began absent-mindedly flipping the pages to and fro.

"Ozier's forgotten that he hasn't had lunch, I think," he said. "I'll rout him out, if you'll excuse me for a moment," and he left the room.

Eliot just then had got into difficulties with the sweet, a tottery affair of macaroons and apricots of which he sent one bastion flying to the floor. In trying to save it the maid nearly deposited the whole on his head. Altogether by the time the remains were removed, Eliot's trouser leg mopped, and at least a fragment of the sweet on his plate, some minutes had passed. Eliot was much amused, and Sebastian had laughed and helped with a will. When all was right again, Eliot turned to Robina Miller with a laughing excuse for his clumsiness, but he did not say the words.

Her lips were pinched together, her cheeks blazing. Her fingers were just being lifted from the little diary which Dawnay had laid down by his plate between himself and her. On her face was a look of repressed fury which there was no mistaking.

Sebastian was saying a word to Morley, the parlourmaid, about really preferring rice pudding, but being sure that macaroon trifle was better for him, and so following the path of virtue but Dawnay came in at that moment.

"No use," he said, sitting down again, and this time pocketing the little diary notebook. "Newton says he must keep his eye on the apple for a few minutes longer. You don't mind, I hope," he said to Robina.

She made an indifferent reply. He looked up sharply at the tone of her voice. He met her eye, and he positively started. Morley was always complaining about Miss Miller being so "difficult," and he knew that she was not an easy-going little thing like his sister Claire. But those blazing eyes—that face—looked distinctly unpleasant.

What had Eliot or Sebastian been saying? If it was Sebastian—surely it was—

The telephone rang. There was an extension in almost every room of his house. He reached for the instrument and listened. "Speaking," he replied to some query, "and who are you? Oh, yes—Mallinson. Quite! . . . At three instead of four? Certainly. Suit me equally well. Would you mind coming round to the summer-house when you get here?" He gave instructions as to how to find this. Not at all," he wound up cordially, "not at all. Pleasure," He replaced the receiver.

The door opened and Dr. Ozier came in. He was a slender man of between thirty and forty, with an eager rapt face. He and Eliot were introduced and Ozier dropped into a chair with a smile at Robina, to which, however, she did not respond. She rose with some murmured apology and left the room with an air of suppressed fury.

Ozier stared inquiringly at his friend and host. "I hope it isn't my being so outrageously late that's made any trouble?"

"Good Lord, no!" came from Dawnay. "I don't know what it is, but I do know that it's not that. Much more likely to be some crime of Morley's. The two don't hit it off well." There were no servants in the room at the moment.

Ozier helped himself meditatively to some tomatoes from the sideboard. He looked, and was, miles away in spirit.

"We've had Morley for years. She's my wife's own maid really and devoted to her," Dawnay went on to Eliot. "She's a privileged person in the house. Hallo, Clare! That window isn't supposed to be unlocked!"

The green velvet curtains had parted, and Clare Dawnay, pretty as a pink-and-white daisy, and with about as much character in her face, stood there.

"I'll shut it," Sebastian Dawnay said promptly.

It shut with a patent catch so that when shut it could not be opened from the outside.

"I found it standing open," Clare said, shaking hands with Eliot and screwing up her face at the idea of lunch. She sat down beside him, only to drift out into the garden with him a moment later to look at Sebastian's car.

Dawnay turned to the butler. "Weatherall, the Mr. Mallinson whom I told you I was expecting at four is coming at three instead. I've told him how to find me in the summer-house, where I shall be working."

"What about our coffee and sherry out there now," Ozier suggested. "I don't want any lunch thanks. By the way, Weatherall, do you know what's become of that old album of snapshots which I use to keep my trays even, in the bath-room?"

Weatherall did not seem to understand for a moment.

"It's one of those you gave me, Charles," Ozier went on to his host, "when I asked for something big and heavy. One of the pile has gone, and my trays won't stand even"

"It was Mr. Sebastian, sir," Weatherall now said. He was a pleasant-looking, middle-aged man with an honest, conscientious face "And I'm afraid he's had an accident with it. He must have dropped a match on, it without noticing, and it all blazed up. Dreadful smell there was in his room this morning, and the album past saving. Burnt to tinder, sir"

Dawnay looked keenly at the butler, seemed as though about to speak, but said nothing, only grinding but the stub of his cigarette with an air of deep concentration before assenting to Ozier's suggestion about the coffee and sherry out of doors.

Ozier sauntered on out, and, as he did so, Sebastian came back and helped himself to a whisky and soda. He began to talk about the car, and looking at him Charles felt more than ever the impossibility of Edie's being right, even though he had been careless with one of the many photographic albums left by his father, that indefatigable photographer. Of course he was Sebastian! Older. Weather-beaten, journey-stained, but still Sebastian. Eliot had "passed" him. Still, he would test him all the same, if only to allay Edie's suspicions for ever. He brought the talk round to Trenders, the old home of the Dawnays, and he dropped quite a neat question as to a secret passage known only to the sons of the house, since one of them had discovered it some thirty years ago. It was not one of his two real tests. With a laugh that showed his strong teeth, Sebastian went into details. And then, Charles put another question as to the mongrel which Sebastian had sent in for a local dog show, as a "Persian hound." With a roar of laughter, Sebastian went into details about that entry too, and, on the instant, catching his laughing, bright eyes on himself, Charles felt a sudden certainty that Edie was right, that this man was not Sebastian at all. More, that he had seen this face—which was not that of Sebastian's—somewhere, sometime in the past.

Rising, he planted his knuckles on the table top, and stared at the other man. Sebastian stared back, his lips tight again, his eyes wary.

"Where have I seen you before?" Charles asked.

Thrusting his hands deep into his pockets, Sebastian faced him.

"What do you mean?" he demanded, and something in the low voice and the hard face staring back at him made

Charles pause. He did not want a row on his hands just when his wits should be at their best to tackle the Lyall affair as it should be tackled. He must get that off the stocks first. He had been a fool to show the so-called cousin his doubts.

"This morning," he went on, "in the City. I waved to you, but I'm dashed if I can remember where it was."

Charles thought that he had carried it off splendidly, and on Sebastian saying that he had not been in the City, he laughed and turned away. If he had seen the look on the other man's face at that moment he might not have felt so pleased with himself.

CHAPTER THREE

PUNCTUALLY at four, Mallinson drove up to Regency Avenue. As he got out of his car, a man closed the gate behind himself. Mallinson recognised him as the man who had touched Dawnay on the arm that morning and suggested his going back with him to see some papers. The stranger lifted his hat politely. He was tall and very well dressed. "Mr. Mallinson?" he asked in a quick, well-bred voice. "On your way in to see our friend Dawnay, I suppose. Unfortunately, you won't find him. He's been trying to reach you for the last half-hour on the telephone."

"Indeed?" Mallinson gave him an inquiring look.

"Yes, he asked me to wait for you and make his excuses. He's had to shift your interview to four, on Wednesday, He's been sent for on some of his Special Committees which wouldn't allow him to delay a moment. By the way, my name is Richards, Colonel Richards." Something in his gaze suggested that the name must be well known. Mallinson met it coldly.

"Am I to understand that Dawnay has just given you a message for me?" he asked formally.

Colonel Richards looked impatient. "Precisely. He asks you to put off your appointment with him till Wednesday at the same hour—four. Now suppose you let me drive you back in my bus—"

He nodded towards a magnificent Rolls some way down. "I've wanted a chat with you for some time about some business which we want you to take up for us. Good business too, if I may say so—" He had Mallinson genially by the elbow, and was trying to turn him round. "We want you to act for us in a coming prosecution—"

Mallinson twisted his elbow free. "Sorry. But I want to leave a message at the house. I feel sure that Dawnay would have left me a line, however hurried he was. I must find out for certain," and he opened the gate.

"He didn't leave any message for you except the verbal one given me," Colonel Richards said firmly. "He—like me—was in a tearing hurry. Something quite unexpected had cropped up But since we have met by chance like this I want you, Mallinson, to come along with me and allow us to lay our case before you. It'll be an expensive proposition, but we don't grudge fees." Again the hand cupped Mallinson s elbow persuasively, bringing a pressure to bear on it which was as much moral as physical.

But Mallinson preferred to bring pressure on other people, not to suffer it. Again he freed himself.

"Not just now," he said firmly. "I want to write a note and leave it for Mr. Dawnay, since he can't see me for the moment. Wednesday is no good to me—" and again he faced the house. This time Colonel Richards let him go. It would have needed violence to stop him; the colonel's face looked as though the idea of force occurred to him, even appealed to him, but was reluctantly given up.

"Sorry," he murmured. "The business unfortunately can't wait. They telephoned me, while I was with Dawnay, that it must be put in hand at once. Immediately."

"Then, as you say, I'm afraid I'm definitely not available." Mallinson by this time was skirting the thick shrubbery, which billowed out like a sail, a line of low annuals outlining it. Evidently the garden proper was on the other side of the shrubs. Colonel Richards, with a snort, wheeled round and made for his car—rather quickly. Mallinson glanced at his watch as he pressed the bell. It showed exactly two minutes to four. He gave his card to the butler and asked for Mr. Charles Dawnay, who was expecting him.

The man looked puzzled. He said that his master was probably still in the summer-house, and would Mr. Mallinson please follow him. He led the way around the end of the house, to a sort of deep pocket made by the green wall of shrubbery. Here, a thatched roof showed above a long oval flower-bed which served to screen it from sight. Beyond was a beautifully kept lawn and a rose pergola.

The thatched roof belonged to the summer-house, whose glass doors stood wide open. So well was the little house placed, so planted was the oval bed with delphiniums and double hollyhocks, tall lupins and towering bushes of michaelmas daisies, that at any season you might have thought yourself in the heart of the country.

"This way, sir," the butler repeated. He put a foot on to the brick floor inside, and gave an exclamation. So did Mallinson, who was close behind him. Both men jumped forward. The body of Charles Dawnay lay half across the table. Blood covered the face like a dark red veil, and lay in a pool on table and floor. It was fairly dry, Mallinson noticed. Dawnay was quite dead.

At that moment Eliot appeared. He had gone for a stroll in the garden after lunch and had forgotten coffee entirely when a particularly good phrase had occurred to him. He had gone to his room to jot it down and had stayed there working.

"Is it better never than late?" he began cheerily. He stopped. The jauntiness fell from him; eyes wide, jaw dropped, he stood staring. "Is he—is he—When did he do it? " he asked stupidly.

"Is there a telephone out here?" Mallinson asked the butler, paying no, heed to Eliot.

With a shaking finger, the butler pointed to a corner by the door.

"Then use it—call Scotland Yard," Mallinson directed.

The butler had to step carefully to avoid the blood on the floor. He lifted the receiver.

"Scotland Yard. Quick!" he croaked. Then, a minute later, he said urgently: "Mr. Charles Dawnay is lying dead in the summer-house of 13 Regency Avenue, St.

John's Wood, with his head battered in. . . . My name? It's
the butler speaking—Weatherall by name. Certainly, sir.
Nothing has been touched, or will be, I assure you. There
are two gentlemen here with me. They'll wait too. You're
coming at once? We shall be very glad to have you here!"
And he hung up.

"I think we might wait outside," Mallinson said and
the man followed him out with alacrity. As for Eliot, he
stepped outside again with the feeling of being in a
dream. The butler seemed to share this feeling.

"It's—well, I can't realise it," he murmured He looked
as if he could not. "It was a savage blow, yon. Cracked his
head in like an egg-shell." And he fell silent.

Mallinson said nothing. He walked impatiently round
the screen of flowers and watched the road. Eliot
followed. He was about to speak when a motor cycle
whizzed by along the road, with one man riding pillion.
Both driver and passenger were in cycling clothes, but
Eliot guessed them to be the police advance-guard. They
stopped at the entrance gate, out of sight of the summer-
house.

"I think the police have come," Mallinson said over his
shoulder to the butler. "I'll go and meet them."

"That's my place, sir," Weatherall said firmly, and cut
around the house before Mallinson could head him off.

Mallinson returned to Eliot and the terrace on which
the summer-house stood. They had not long to wait. A
man in motor-cycling rig came round the summer-house.
He stopped dead at sight of the two men.

"Where is the butler?" Mallinson asked. "He brought
me out here."

The constable did not reply, he viewed any person on
the scene of a crime with distrust. However, neither
Mallinson nor Eliot seemed to have bloodstains on them.
The constable unbent so far as to ask the solicitor.

"Friend of his, sir?"

"No," Mallinson replied, "acquaintance merely"

"Same here," replied Eliot, "though I'm staying at the house."

The group suddenly stiffened to attention as they heard a car draw up. Then, after a moment, steps, many steps, came swiftly along the gravel on the other side of the hedge. One more minute and the butler appeared, with a tall, well set-up man who gave the waiting two one swift glance from a pair of steady, dark grey eyes. For the rest, he had regular features, and a grave, very reserved expression which went well with the strength of the jaw and the cut of a firm mouth.

Eliot stepped forward with an exclamation of pleasure. This was Chief Inspector Pointer, the man who had had so much to do with his cousin, Martin Blair, over the Joan Ingilby affair. Blair had shared Eliot's flat before the end of the trial, and Eliot had got to know the chief inspector really well. And to know Pointer was to like him—unless you were a crook, when to meet him was disaster. And suddenly, as he felt his hand grasped in the remembered grip, firm, friendly, warm and certain, Eliot felt that whatever came it would not be a nightmare, but something well worth watching. His first impulsive question as to whether Dawnay had killed himself had been instantly replaced by the knowledge that Dawnay had been murdered. And with that knowledge something horrible, because out of the normal, had seemed to engulf the house; but it was lifted now, or at least pushed back.

Mallinson introduced himself in his usual brisk, competent, business-like way, but gave no explanation of his presence. Here was a man, Eliot thought, who took murders and death as part of the day. Probably solicitors who dealt much with Wills got to feel like that. He thought that he would like to make a film some day depicting a family of four sons, each originally very like the other, and each in the end changed entirely by their different professions.

All this only took a moment, then Pointer, asking the men to stay where they were for a moment, took his hat

off and stepped through the glass doors into the summer-
house itself. He was followed by the police doctor, and
some other men who had come with him.

He found himself in a square little room with a red
brick floor and pine-panelled walls. A thick rug lay in the
centre, on which stood a knee-hole writing-table. There
were many shelves across one end, a cocktail cabinet
against one wall, two chairs with gay cretonne cushions,
and a wooden chair with a rounded back to it, on which
the dead man was sitting. The doctor was bending over
the table.

"Humph!" murmured the doctor, "cause of death is
certainly simple enough. Head bashed in."

The camera clicked a few times. Then the Yard
photographer stepped away.

"Any sign that he was drugged as well?" Pointer
asked.

The doctor scrutinised the pupils and shook his head.
"Nothing suggests it." He bent over the wound. "Done
with something round . . . size of a large apple. . . . Any
idea what did it?" he asked the chief inspector.

"Nothing that I can see here fits the wound," Pointer
said. He motioned to the butler. "Look in, but don't come
in. Anything taken from here?" he asked him. "We're
looking for a possible weapon. Something in the nature of
a club probably."

The man looked instantly at the walls of the house.

"Gipsy Joe's cudgel's gone!" he exclaimed in a tone of
horror. "It hangs there over the oil radiator by its thong.
You could fell an ox with it."

"And Gipsy Joe?" Pointer asked.

"He's a chap who threatened Mr. Dawnay only last
week. Mr. Dawnay ran over his dog on a dark night. It
was that, or old Mrs. Blotter, and he had to chance the
dog. There's no denying that Gipsy Joe fair worshipped
that dog. Mr. Dawnay was ever so sorry, but there wasn't
anything he could do."

"But this cudgel that's missing?" Pointer prompted.

"He had it with him when he came up here to see Mr. Dawnay," Weatherall said meaningly "He just came to make a row. He had refused the compensation offered him. He just brought that there cudgel—some ten days ago it would be now—pushed past me and tramped round here to the simmer-house where Mr. Dawnay was working over some papers. I don't know what happened, Mr. Dawnay sent me back to the house, but I can guess, for Gipsy Joe hasn't shown, up since, and Mr. Dawnay had barked knuckles when he hung up that there cudgel on a nail an hour or so later. He was whistling as he did so. Rare pleased he looked. And he says to me 'Tell Mr. Gipsy Joseph Waters that he can have that back again any time he likes to ask me for it personally, you understand?' And he gives me a wicked grin. I says as how I perfectly understood, which I did. Mr. Dawnay wasn't the kind of gentleman that any one could hunt with a cudgel and expect to get away with it." Weatherall's tone was of affectionate pride.

"Do either of you know the man in question?" Pointer asked two constables who had been sent up from the nearest police station.

"Chap of the name of Joseph Waters? Yes, sir. Always called Gipsy Joe from his looks."

"About how long ago would you think he was murdered?" Pointer asked the doctor, who was expecting the question.

"It's a quarter-past four now." They all drew out their watches. "Well, around about an hour ago, I should say."

"Round about an hour ago?" Pointer repeated, and the doctor nodded.

"Near as no matter."

Pointer turned to the constable. "Then find out what this man Waters was doing from about half-past two to four. Or if that's not possible, then from three to four."

The man saluted and hurried away.

While his fingerprint men were at work, Pointer stepped out again on to the lawn.

"Now, sir," he asked the young solicitor first, will you tell me just how you came to find the body?"

Mallinson explained that he had come for a chat with the dead man at four o'clock and had been shown to the summer-house, to find what the chief inspector saw before him.

"A friend of his?"

Mallinson repeated that he was only an acquaintance, that Dawnay and he had met by chance in the City that morning and had fallen into talk. And that Dawnay had asked him drop in this afternoon around four.

"But I thought you was to come at three, sir," put in the butler.

Mallinson stared at him inquiringly.

"The master said a gentleman of the name of Mallinson was coming at four; then later he said to me 'Mr. Mallinson is coming at three, not four. See that no one disturbs us.'"

Mallinson shook his head with a look of bewilderment.

"I didn't change the hour. I've only just come! But I found a Colonel Richards just leaving, who told me that Dawnay had to go out, and had given him a message for me to say that our interview was to be put off till Wednesday. He did his best to make sure that I shouldn't go on up to the house," Mallinson added with some warmth.

Weatherall gaped.

"Did you show any one in at three?" Pointer asked him.

"No, sir. Mr. Dawnay was in the summer-house, and he generally tells people how to go straight there—that is, if he wants to see them."

"How many visitors have there been this afternoon besides this gentleman?"

"Not one, sir. No one has rung the front door bell except him. I think Miss Clare has a visitor, but she must have met him in the garden and brought him in herself."

"Do you know Colonel Richards, sir? His address?"
Pointer asked Mallinson, who said that he did not, that
he had only once seen the man before, and that was this
morning, when in the City he had jumped out of a smart
car and tried to buttonhole Mr. Dawnay.

Weatherall repeated that no one—colonel or plain
mister—had rung the front door bell.

There was no time to thrash this out at the moment,
important though it sounded. Eliot was next asked how
he came to be at the house, and what brought him out to
the summer-house? As he explained in full, he felt
uneasily conscious that, had he been a stranger, his
explanations might have sounded thin. Fortunately he
had no motive to slay Charles Dawnay, and that being so,
a sudden overwhelming curiosity took possession of him
to find out who had.

The doctor had now finished his first, preliminary
examination, and had a word to say to Pointer about the
P.M. arrangements, then he picked up his bag and left.
Chairs were brought for Mallinson and Eliot, in case
there was anything more which must be asked of them at
once, and Inspector Watts, a quiet, small, keen-eyed man,
and the chief inspector stepped back again into the
summer-house. Mallinson's chair had been placed, as he
noticed, on the other side of the bed of flowers, so that he
could neither hear nor see anything of what went on
behind them. But the butler was asked to go in with the
two detective officers and tell them whether anything
more beside the cudgel was missing, or had had its
position altered, or whether anything had been added to
the room.

Weatherall looked about him very carefully.

"Where are the two sherry glasses from the lunch
table?" he asked finally. "They were brought out here
after lunch, yet they aren't anywhere about that I can
see"

Nor that the others could see, either.

"May I open the doors of the cocktail cabinet to look?" the butler asked.

Pointer handed him a pair of rubber gloves. "We shall have to have your fingerprints, of course," he said, "but even so, it will save work if you'll pull these on." The butler did so and swung the door open.

"Here are the two glasses. Cleaned!" He puzzled. "That's funny. I know they're the dining-room ones that were used, because they're the grape-vine pattern. We use an odd lot of older ones for out here." He pointed to a corner fitment. "There's a sink in there where the master washes his hands after doing a bit of gardening. That's where these glasses must have been washed. And wiped with the hand-towel," he added, picking a glass up and looking through it. "Covered with lint!"

He opened the cupboard. They saw a fitted basin with a tap, and a towel-rail to one side above it. The towel was put back untidily.

"How would any one know there was water there?" Pointer asked, for, when shut, the cupboard looked like the one on the opposite side which held shelves and books. "Did it stand open often?"

"Not to my knowledge, sir. Mr. Dawnay always shut it. Very tidy gentleman, the master, sir."

"To the point of washing up his own wine glasses?" Pointer asked dryly.

The butler looked shocked. "Oh, no, sir! Why should he? The speaking tube through to the house is in perfect order. Besides, there are these others ready for use. Very odd I call it."

So did Pointer. But here again he must let side-issues wait.

"Was the master poisoned before he was struck down?" Weatherall asked suddenly. "That there Gipsy Joe knows alot of funny herbs—I mean herbs that don't mean no good to any one. He grows them in his back garden; plants no one else has ever seen the like of."

"Why do you think Mr. Dawnay might have been poisoned?" Pointer asked.

"Just wondering, sir. Those washed glasses and then, the master wasn't the kind to sit still and let any one crack him over the head. I mean, it looks to me as if the Gipsy had done it by a trick, and he knows some funny ones!"

Pointer had to let this too rest for the present.

"Who is staying at the house just now?"

"Only Mr. Sebastian Dawnay, the master's cousin, home on holiday from South Africa, and Doctor Ozier, the master's greatest friend. He's here for a fortnight. And Mr. Eliot, who writes for the films."

"Is Doctor Ozier in the house now?"

"Yes, sir. At least I think he is. It's a safe guess that he's at his tubes and spirit lamps and microscopes."

"Then why didn't you fetch him when you found Mr. Dawnay dead?"

Weatherall's jaw dropped.

"I never thought of it!" he said, with what looked like honest surprise, and disgust at his own dullness. "I never thought of his being a real doctor! I never thought of him at all in this—"

It sounded genuine, but Pointer reserved his judgment.

"And this Miss Clare you spoke of?"

"Oh, she's just the master's sister, sir. Quite young is Miss Clare. And a nasty shock this will be to her, let alone to Mrs. Dawnay!"

"Where is Mrs. Dawnay, now?"

Weatherall explained about the children and the scarlet fever, and Cromer.

Pointer was thankful to know that for the time being she was out of the house—and the murder.

"Miss Miller, a relative of the master's, has come to look after things while the mistress is away. She's a young lady as is studying Domestic Science at some classes. She's in the house, of course."

"How can one reach Mrs. Dawnay at once?" Pointer wanted to know, and Weatherall handed him her address at Cromer.

Pointer was done with the summerhouse for the time being, and left it in charge of one of his men while he stepped around the flowers again and looked about him.

CHAPTER FOUR

THE chief inspector stood looking carefully about him. He saw the green walls of thick shrubs, the oval bed lying like a curved bar in front of the summer-house, locking it away into seclusion.

"A man could be murdered in there, within sound of the road and the pavement, and yet no one but the flying birds see it done," Mallinson was saying to Eliot.

"Gipsy Joe swore he would get that cudgel of his back." The butler considered that in the presence of death all men are equal. "So they say at the Churchill Arms, where I sometimes drops in for a chat with the proprietor." Weatherall was very genteel. "He has right, enough! That cudgel of his would have brained an ox. And after it was done, he could slip it up his coat, or down the back of it."

"You think he took it away with him? I wonder!"

Pointer had rubber gloves on. Taking out his knife, he stepped forward on to the bed and cut the green encircling string which tied a very luxuriant Michaelmas daisy into a cabbage-like bunch. He felt among the flopping greenery released by his knife, and drew out a cudgel which had been stuck upright in the soft earth. Then he stepped back, scuffling his footprints away by a green stick which stood among some heucheras.

The butler was quite overcome by what he considered a marvellous example of lightning like deduction on the part of the C.I.D. officer, he ever after maintained that for Mr. Pointer, after merely hearing about the cudgel and Gipsy Joe, to step at once to the right plant, plunge his hand in, and draw out the weapon, savoured of second sight.

"Gipsy Joe's cudgel! And found by you in a tick, sir!" he muttered in awe.

But it really had been elementary. Dawnay employed a first-class gardener; everything in his garden, the way each piece of work was done, spoke for this. Yet in the oval bed one large plant, a Michaelmas daisy, was tied in a fashion quite unlike any of the other plants. A stick to a spray is a gardener's motto, and the tie crossed between the stick and the plant. Here some one had roughly cut the old ties, thrust something into the centre of the mass and re-tied the whole plant very much as an Italian wine grower ties bass together over the top of a wine bottle.

The fingerprint man was trying the handle with great care, but it had also been thrust into the ground, probably before the club was placed upright, and unfortunately the bed had been well watered that morning.

"Sort of thing Gipsy Joe would think of," said the butler when he heard about the lack of fingerprints and the cause of it. "He's as clever as a weasel!"

"Is he good at gardening?" asked Pointer, eyeing the clutter of tangled raffia.

"Very—when he feels like it, sir," said the butler. "That's his cudgel right enough"

Pointer swung the cudgel thoughtfully to and fro, knocking the dirt off it. It was a formidable weapon, and wonderfully balanced. Even a woman could have used it, especially if she were familiar with the use of Indian clubs.

Yes, it would make just such a wound as had killed Dawnay. The dust under Dawnay's fingers, the first three fingers of his right hand . . . it might well be that he had stooped to pick something up from the brick floor and the murderer had taken that opportunity to fell him. For now that he had the cudgel, Pointer believed that the blow had been struck by some one standing in front of the dead man, not from behind him. Gipsy Joe? Certainly a better place for a blood-stained club than soft garden soil could not have been found. Had the Michaelmas daisy been carefully tied, it might have remained there for weeks.

Meanwhile Eliot felt a bitter disappointment. Was this the end? A gipsy's revenge for a runover dog? And here he was just waking to the thrill of pitting his brains against an abnormal man—for a murderer is abnormal, and abnormally conceited too, for apart from any other deterrents, he must imagine that he can get away with his crime, or he wouldn't commit murder. In a flash Eliot realised what it would be to work with Pointer on a case, with he himself staying in the very house where the murder had occurred—in the house, Dawnay's house, where he had felt such funny undercurrents a few hours ago. All this would count for nothing if this strolling vagabond had done the murder, but it might have been vital if the crime had been a cleverly planned affair. The injustice of his fate rankled. He had never been near a murder before except as Martin Blair's cousin, and now, when he had been given a front-row seat, the murder was not worth recording. He had liked Charles Dawnay. He had in these last silent minutes seen himself translating that liking into action . . . . big and important . . . his spirit saying to the spirit of the dead man: "Rest in peace. I have avenged you."

That sort of thing. . . . And then the explanation to prove so ridiculously unexciting.

"Quick work," Mallinson murmured to him. "A murder—Scotland Yard called in—an immediate solution."

He looked surprised at the sulky nod that his congratulatory words got in answer.

"You're a writer, you say," Mallinson went on. "Of course that's different. You can work in the middle of the night probably as well as in the daytime, if not better. Commercial Law's my speciality —Company Law—and our time's strictly limited. Lord knows I had earmarked this afternoon for a stack of papers that's got to be waded through before night."

Pointer asked them and the butler to come back to the house.

Weatherall showed them into the dining-room, where a plain clothes man sat writing at a table, and got them each a whisky and soda. That done, Pointer had Weatherall take him to the telephone. The house had two; one with many extensions, the other in Dawnay's study, which was really private. Pointer telephoned to the hotel in Cromer. Was Mrs. Dawnay there? He was told that the lady in question had sent word that she would arrive in time for dinner at eight. The children and the nurses had come by the noon train.

Pointer asked to speak to the head nurse. Could she tell him how to get into touch with Mrs. Dawnay? It was very important . . . very urgent.

The woman thought that he had better try Mrs. Dawnay's town house—she gave the number. Mrs. Dawnay had got out of the train at the next stopping place after they had started, saying that she had some shopping to do and would not be at Cromer until the evening.

Pointer tried to get some other suggestions out of the woman without alarming her, but he eventually had to hang up without securing any more helpful information. Apparently Mrs. Dawnay could not be told of the tragedy until she should arrive at the hotel that evening

He explained how things were to Weatherall, who appeared surprised. "Mrs. Dawnay told me she was going down with the children and the nurses by train," the butler said, puzzled, "getting there around four. She's not a lady to change her plans easily, either. The master thought so too, I know, for he happened to say something to Doctor Ozier at lunch about Mrs. Dawnay and the children having a jolly view at that very moment from the train windows."

"Ah, Doctor Ozier! Take me to his room, please. I ought to see him next."

"May I come?" Eliot had found inaction impossible. "1 won't butt in. But may I come?"

Pointer had liked Eliot. He had found him clever and reliable, and quite good at the few bits of detective work he had given him when he was working on the case in which Eliot's cousin had been concerned. If this were not Gipsy Joe—and Pointer by no means accepted that theory as yet—then Eliot's being in the house, knowing the people, might be of the greatest use. And besides, Pointer remembered his zeal. Eliot unemployed by him would be Eliot off hunting on his own. He might do a lot of damage without intending to, and the Yard might lose a very useful helper.

"By all means Eliot, I should like you to," were the welcome words that took Eliot swiftly up the stairs beside the taller man.

Weatherall led the way up and knocked at a door. "If he's at his experiments he doesn't like to have the door opened too suddenly," he explained.

There was no answer. Weatherall turned the knob quietly, and stepped in.

"Oh, my Lord!" This last, unorthodox, remark on entering the room was due to the sight of the figure of a man lying curled up on the floor in front of an arm-chair.

The butler would have jumped to his side, but a grip of steel held him back.

"Stand where you are for a moment!" came from the chief inspector, as he and Eliot bent over the man. The long thin face was a livid grey, with purple shadows in the eye sockets. There was a look around the mouth that made Pointer put a hand swiftly to the man's heart. He thought that it was beating; but that was all that he could say.

The man's knees were drawn up to his chest, but the look on his face was one of deep peace. His shoes seemed to interest the chief inspector. The soles showed gravel marks and stains of crushed thyme flowers, crimson thyme such as grew in the crevices of the crazy paving around the summer-house.

Pointer studied the soles of his own and Eliot's shoes. They were both like those of the unconscious man.

"Two of them!" came from Weatherall by the door. "Doctor Ozier and the master!"

"He's not dead yet," Pointer told him. "There's a telephone near you, Eliot. Telephone to the nearest police station to send their doctor, will you. And as for you—" he spoke to Weatherall again, "be on hand in the hall downstairs to let the doctor in and bring him up here. But be very careful not to let any one in the house know what has happened. Keep out of everybody's way as much as you can."

Weatherall promised to obey to the letter, and went on down. A whistle from Pointer brought a young plain clothes man up three steps at a time. He was left beside the unconscious man, while Pointer, followed by Eliot, went over the other rooms. The servants' rooms were on the floor above.

The only other occupant up there seemed to be behind a locked door. On their gently trying the handle, the voice of Robina Miller called out that no one could come in.

After going over the other rooms and finding them empty, Pointer, followed by his new assistant, went on to the ground floor. Pointer himself opened the first door, that of the drawing-room. Clare Dawney was standing at the farther end, facing the door. She was clasping and unclasping her hands.

"I daren't! I can't! Don't ask me!" came quiveringly, from her trembling lips. She had a charmingly pretty face, blonde and childish, but at the moment terrified-looking. Enough of a pair of long legs and arms could be seen outside of an easy-chair, facing her, to make out that a man sat in it.

"If you try, you can!" came sharply from the chair.

Pointer closed the door without a sound.

"Who are they?" he asked when at a safe distance.

"She's Dawnay's sister. I don't know his voice."

Pointer had a word with Weatherall and the butler glided off, to come back a moment later, to report that the gentleman in question was a Mr. Lyall, a distant connection of the Dawnays.

"How did he get in?" Pointer asked.

He was told that "The young lady must have brought him in along with her. She frequently does." Weatherall's tone was significant, but the chief inspector had no time just then for anything but the main bones of the affair.

"Do those baize doors lead to the servants' wing?" he asked, and was told that his guess was correct.

Leaving Eliot, Pointer slipped through them, and along a passage to where he heard voices. Pushing the door cautiously ajar, he found the four women servants having tea in a white-tiled kitchen. Evidently no news of the murder had reached here.

Pointer slipped back along the passage as a car could be heard driving in. He took the stairs two at a time, but, even so, he was barely ahead of the local police doctor, a stocky man who seemed in a tearing hurry. He fell upon the unconscious man like a dog on a bone, and began pulling him round to the light.

The room and the man had already been photographed, in case it should be necessary to know just how he was lying.

Pointer introduced himself.

"Doctor Melville," the newcomer muttered, as he began pulling Ozier's lids open, and examining his eyeballs; "He's been dosed. Narcotic of some kind," he said next, "or else he's taken something. Not much chance of pulling him through. Can't think what it is. . . ." He sniffed at the mouth, examined the eyeballs again, and reflexed the arms and legs. "Doesn't act like anything I know," he said finally. "There's a nursing home across the way. I'll take him along there and get to work on him. It's his only chance, though his heart may give out before we get him there."

Pointer told one of his men to help the doctor and Weatherall to carry the unconscious man down the stairs and into the car at the steps. As they did so, Pointer heard Miss Miller's voice through her closed door.

"Is it the piano?" she asked. "I telephoned them I had changed my mind about having it taken downstairs. Mrs. Dawnay can see to it when she returns, Weatherall."

Weatherall made no reply.

Walter Lyall came out at the sound of the scuffling feet. He took a step forward as the men and their burden reached the hall.

"Why, it's Ozier! What on earth—"

"Taken an overdose of something, or some of his experiments have made him unconscious," Pointer said briskly. His glance just flickered to Clare. Lyall turned his head.

"Go back into the drawing-room, darling, I'll join you in a minute," he said peremptorily.

Clare obediently turned, twittering, "Oh," and "Oh dear!" and "How dreadful!" breathlessly. Mallinson, hearing Lyall's voice, came out of the room where he had been most impatiently waiting.

"You've heard?" he began "You know about poor Dawnay, of course!" Then he stopped. "You don't! Or at least you look as though you don't." Rather an odd correction, Pointer thought. It suggested a lack of transparency on the part of the man to whom it was addressed, and a knowledge of this little foible on the part of the speaker.

"Come in here!" Mallinson pulled Lyall into the room behind him. Pointer came in too.

Mallinson at once turned. "Sorry, chief inspector," he said civilly. "I want a word with this gentleman alone."

"But so do I, Mr. Mallinson," Pointer said blandly. "At least, I don't care about its being alone. Why should he know that Mr. Dawnay is dead?"

His eyes rested casually on the stranger as he spoke. The young man, or, rather, youngish man, certainly looked horrified and amazed.

"Somehow one expected the very roof to cry it aloud," Mallinson said, to that. "But let me introduce you—Chief Inspector Pointer from New Scotland Yard—Mr. Lyall—a cousin of Mr. Dawnay's."

"Third cousin, to be precise," Walter said promptly. "And now, will you please explain? What's happened to Charles? What killed him? When?"

Pointer told him what had been found in the summer-house. Lyall certainly seemed amazed and horrified. "I suppose Mrs. Dawnay is completely overcome?"

So he was not an intimate of the household.

"We can't get into touch with Mrs. Dawnay at present." Pointer explained the difficulty. Could Mr. Lyall help?

But Lyall had no idea where the lady could be found if she was not at Cromer. "I dare, Miss Dawnay will know where she is. I'll ask her at once."

Lyall started for the door, but Pointer interposed.

"A moment! Do you know anything of a certain Colonel Richards?" he asked.

Lyall looked surprised. "You mean the Islas Secretary? I know him by sight—"

"The Secretary of the Islas del Rio Syndicate!" Mallinson's voice was that of a man who sees a light in the dark.

"What of it?" Lyall's tone was impatient

"This of it," Mallinson said with a sarcastic calm, "that he either killed Doctor Ozier and Charles Dawnay, or he's at least in the crime. He did his damndest not to have the two murders discovered at once. Of course!" His eye sought Pointer's. "The doctor wasn't quite dead, you said? Evidently Richards' plan was to play for time and safety."

It looked like it, they all agreed.

Pointer promptly asked for Colonel Richards' telephone number, then stepped out into the hall and handed it to Inspector Watts. He himself sent a code message to the Yard for particulars of the man and his company.

CHAPTER FIVE

POINTER turned away from the telephone to speak to Eliot, who was hovering around, and they both saw tall, broad-shouldered Sebastian Dawnay come round from the garage. He stared at the sight of the men hoisting the unconscious Ozier into a car.

They heard him exclaim "Good God, what's happened?"

Sebastian Dawnay's light, predatory eyes went from the chief inspector to the butler. There was a slight likeness to the dead man in face and figure, Pointer thought, but this Dawnay looked a tough customer. The kind to grab what he wanted with no uncertain hand. His wants would probably be rather crude.

Pointer introduced himself, though he had a shrewd idea that Sebastian had guessed who he was. Those light eyes were very intelligent eyes.

Pointer told him of his summons to the house and what he had found there. Sebastian's face showed every mark of horror and shock, but he said nothing for a moment. Then:

"Have you let Mrs. Dawnay know?"

Pointer explained that he would only too gladly do so but he had no idea where the lady was.

"Cromer." Sebastian mentioned the name of the hotel.

Pointer explained still further.

"What a position!" Sebastian said feelingly. "They idolise each other."

The telephone bell rang.

It was from Cromer. The message was that Mrs. Dawnay had just telephoned to say she would not be down until the following morning. Unfortunately, she had hung up before she could herself be spoken to by a slow-witted hall-porter.

Pointer hung up. It was odd, this message. He passed it on to Lyall, who had come out into the hall, too.

"May I ask which of you is now, at least temporarily, the head of the house?" he asked.

Lyall nodded curtly towards Sebastian. "That's your man!" There was something in the gesture which suggested a deeper meaning.

So Sebastian was the heir . . . from South Africa. A good knobkeri would not be at all unlike that cudgel which had hung on the simmer-house wall.

"I think Miss Dawnay should be told what has happened to her brother," Pointer went on

"I'll break it to her. We're engaged," Lyall said promptly, and made for the door.

"Engaged?" Sebastian said curtly. "First I've heard of it."

"Charlie would have told you this evening, had he lived," Lyall said and passed on.

"I understand there is another lady—a Miss Miller—in the house," Pointer said. "I think some one should fetch her. Which is her room?"

"I'll go for her." Sebastian took the stairs four at a time.

"She won't come out of it," he said, coming back almost instantly. "The devil knows what's loose in the house to-day. She refuses to come out."

Pointer went to the room which he knew was Miss Miller's. He left the butler talking to Lyall and Mallinson in the hall. "Gipsy Joe's cudgel," Weatherall was saying. "You, Mr. Sebastian, warned the master not to hang it there. Provocative, you called it, and it's certainly provoked Gipsy Joe right enough! He swore—"

Pointer knocked at a door. As he did so he heard sounds of some one moving to and fro and the rustle of paper.

"Please open the door," he said in a low but very official voice. "I am a detective officer from New Scotland Yard."

The door was opened on the instant. Pointer looked into a pair of startled dark eyes. Behind the young woman he caught a glimpse of a trunk, half packed.

Robina Miller stared at her visitor in what seemed absolute surprise, then she came out.

"What has happened? I had no idea anything was wrong. . . ." She looked below her at Lyall and Mallinson and the butler. Her glance strayed to the open door of Doctor Ozier's room.

"There's been a double accident," Pointer said to Mr. Dawnay and to Doctor Ozier, and with that preliminary, he told her what had happened. She looked stupefied at the news. She acted, if she did not feel, extreme shock.

"And Mrs. Dawnay? Is she downstairs?" she asked finally.

Pointer again explained that as far as he knew the wife was still in ignorance of her husband's death.

The drawing-room door opened and Clare, catching sight of Robina Miller, ran up to her.

"Robina! It can't be true! It can't—" For a moment she sobbed on the elder girl's shoulder. Then she broke out with: "And Edie's away! No one knows where she is. She's not at Cromer."

"No, she's not at Cromer," Miss Miller agreed in a hard voice.

"But we must get into touch with her," Clare urged. "Imagine her shopping, or, having tea, while Charles lies dead! Murdered by that dreadful Gipsy!"

There was a moment's silence, while from below they could hear the three men discussing Gipsy Joe.

Clare turned again to Robina, who stood very erect beside her, a shut-in look on her face. She had a smouldering eye, Pointer thought.

"Robina, can't you think of anything? You can always suggest things!" Clare said almost desperately.

"I shouldn't wonder if Mrs. Dawnay has gone to confession," Robina said at last, speaking slowly and in a certain close-lipped, tight-lipped way, "I shouldn't wonder at all."

"Confession?" Clare stared. "To-day? But—"

There was a short silence. Robina would have turned to Pointer again, but Clare interrupted.

"She usually goes to confession to Father Taunton at the Carmelite Church in Kensington. I wonder! I wonder if she's going to stay at the Carmelite convent! I can't ring up Father Taunton, but I can ring up the convent."

They went downstairs and Clare picked up the telephone. She gave a number. She asked if she could speak to the guest mistress. Was Mrs. Charles Dawnay at the convent by any chance? At the answer she received Clare looked up at Pointer, and at the very still figure beside him.

"She's there! They've gone to fetch her to the phone! But what shall I say to her?" Her lips quivered. "I can't tell her about Charles! I can't!"

Sebastian was standing beside her. Lyall on the other hand had drawn back almost behind Mallinson.

A voice spoke through the telephone. Clare made a sign for silence and listened attentively, then she said falteringly: "Edie, darling, don't get worried or frightened, but Doctor Ozier's ill . . . he's gone to the nursing home close by. Please come home at once; Yes, I'm afraid it must be very serious. . . the doctor thinks so. . . . Good. . . ." She hung up, her face more troubled than ever. "She's coming at once! She'll be here in five minutes or so Robina! You must be the one to tell her."

"No," came instantly, "you, Clare. You're her sister-in-law. I'm only a very distant connexion of Charles'."

"But you must," persisted Clare.

"No, I will not," Robina replied quietly. There was a long pause.

Pointer looked at her steadily. Robina Miller meant what she said. He saw that. This was no attack of nerves.

This was decided on and would be abided by, if her face were any guide to her character. There was in her, the chief inspector felt certain, something of steel, something that could resent fiercely; probably also something that could feel deeply and passionately. There were many capabilities in this young woman.

"Don't worry too much about what to say," Sebastian finally said to Clare, who was crying into her handkerchief. "Edie's any amount of grit in her. It was clever of you to speak as though it were only Ozier who was ill. And a damned funny illness it is too."

Pointer held up his hand. The gate at the end of the drive had clashed shut. A car could be heard driving up.

"It'll be Mrs. Dawnay," murmured the butler, quite unnecessarily.

A taxi drew up as he opened the door. Wide-eyed, Edie Dawnay jumped out.

"Where's Mr. Dawnay?" were her first words to the butler, and "Where's Charles?" to Walter Lyall. Sebastian Dawnay did not seem to exist for her.

"Where's Charles?" she repeated insistently. "Or is he with Vincent?"

Walter Lyall made no reply. Clare went on crying. She had been deeply attached to her brother. She thought the position too poignant to be borne. Edith Dawnay saw her, and gave a cry.

"Something's happened to Charles?" Her eyes were wide with apprehension, her lips white. "It's not Ozier at all, it's Charles!" She took a step towards Clare, who caught her sister-in-law to her with a cry of grief and sympathy.

"Be brave, Edie!" she whispered brokenly.

Edith disengaged herself violently. "He's dead!" The words were a gasp. Her eyes, enormous in her white strained face, looked around her in an unseeing stare.

She was inside the door now, and a maid came running up.

"Oh, Miss Edie—ma'am, I mean—I've just heard! Oh, ma'am!" She caught one of Mrs. Dawnay's ungloved hands in her own. It was pulled away on the instant with a look of utter horror, or was it some emotion darker still? And the odd thing was that Morley, for it was she, fell back silenced.

Pointer looked at each face in the group. There was concern to be read on each, with the exception of Robina Miller's. That young woman's face was very enigmatic as she gazed steadily at the young widow from under her level brows. She made no move to go to her. Eliot, remembering how kindly she had spoken of her, how eagerly she had planned for her, marvelled.

"Take me to him," Edith said next. "What was it? Heart? Where's our doctor?

Pointer stepped forward. She had had all the time that he could allow her before passing on to the last, most terrible truth.

"The doctor is making his examination into the cause of Mr. Dawnay's death at the moment," he said gently. "You can't see him for a little while, I'm sorry to say."

She looked from him to the others, always excepting Sebastian Dawnay, at whom she never once glanced.

"Who are you, pray? What is it you're keeping from me? What is it—? The children!" came in a sudden cry of terror.

"No, no!" Pointer assured her, "they're quite all right. I am Chief Inspector Pointer from New Scotland Yard—" he paused, but Edith Dawnay was too dazed to be able to understand what his words meant. She made a gesture of entreaty and dread which forbade delay, which spoke of being very near breaking point.

"Your husband was found dead in the summerhouse at four this afternoon, Mrs. Dawnay," Pointer, said quietly. "He had been killed by a blow on the head."

"Who was it?" Edith asked Pointer directly in a hard, firm voice.

"Gipsy Joe, madam," came from Weatherall. Edith looked only at Pointer.

"Was it Gipsy Joe?" she demanded in a strangled tone.

"It may have been," Pointer replied evasively. "He certainly seems to have had a grudge against your husband. Do you know of any other enemy that Mr. Dawnay had?"

She stood quite still for a moment. "Open enemy? No," was her curious reply. "But are not a man's foes generally those of his own household? So I can't even see Charles' body!"

"Not for the moment," Pointer had to tell her.

She turned, almost as though lost in thought, towards the stairs. He stopped her.

"I'm sorry to harass you at such a moment, Mrs.Dawnay, please believe that. But when did you last see Mr. Dawnay?"

She went so white that he moved forward, but she stood quite steady.

"This morning around twelve, when he saw us off at the station. Something was troubling me, however, and I decided to have a quiet day at a Carmelite Convent I know well—after doing some shopping. I was there when the telephone message reached me—about Dr. Ozier." And at that she staggered as she turned towards the stairs.

Clare was at her side in a moment, so was Lyall; so for that matter were Pointer, Mallinson, Eliot and Sebastian Dawnay, but she only slipped a hand along Clare's arm, and then on the first step turned:

"Send Morley to me, please."

Morley hurried forward to Mrs. Dawnay's side, but Edith Dawnay pulled away before the other could reach her, with the quite unmistakable intention of avoiding any personal contact.

Morley fell back, and slowly, almost reluctantly, followed Clare and Mrs. Dawnay to a room at the top of

the stairs, a sewing-room. As she stood hesitantly at the
door, Clare came out again, and the others heard her say:

"She wants you—alone, Morley. I hope you'll be able
to help her."

Morley went into the room, and they heard a fierce
"Shut the door and come here!" in a voice of steel. Yet it
was the voice of Edith Dawnay.

CHAPTER SIX

POINTER went out again to the summer-house. Eliot went with him. The constable on duty handed Pointer a list of the articles, which had been taken from the dead man's pockets, and then, saluting, took up an unobtrusive position outside.

Pointer glanced over it and handed it to Eliot to read. Then he looked around the room as though seeking something definite.

"Something missing?" Eliot asked.

Pointer, without replying, finished his quick tour of the little room, which included, opening and closing the cupboard doors, and the drawers of the writing-table. He even lifted the two candlesticks on the mantel and glanced under them. Eliot noticed the drips of sealing wax beside one, freshly made, and a charred wisp of what apparently had been an envelope in the grate. The paper was charred too much to be able to touch it.

"Yes," Pointer said now, "there is something missing. Rather, quaint. Run your eye over the list again and then look around, and see if you can spot what one would have expected to find on him, or near him, and yet which isn't in the room, nor on the list."

Eliot did so. He noticed nothing, and said so.

"Where are his matches?" Pointer, asked. "None in his pockets. None in the summer-house. Yet that candle's been used. Something was sealed. . . . There's a pillar-box not far from his gate—he may have posted something, of which that burnt envelope marks a spoiled effort. I wonder where those matches are. . . . Handed to the man who afterwards murdered him, say for him to light a cigarette?

"He wouldn't hand them to this Gipsy Joe, surely," put in Eliot. He did not know it, but his voice sounded quite hopeful.

"I wonder what Dawnay was stooping for when he was slogged," Pointer said. "His nails show that he was groping around for something on the floor when he was struck down. There's nothing on the floor now—but dust, and blood. Whatever it was has been picked up, unless it was something that has evaporated."

Pointer was emptying the contents of the paper basket into a large envelope and fastening it shut. He placed the envelope in a suitcase which was standing on the table and of which the detective on guard had just handed him the key.

Pointer and Eliot glanced over the dead man's belongings. They seemed of the usual type. He had six or seven pounds on him in notes and change. His note-case had several letters. Nothing to Pointer appeared to have been touched by the murderer, at least there were none of the signs which, to experienced eyes, almost always betrays this fact. Last of all Pointer took up the pocket-diary of the murdered man. It was of a small popular kind, giving a page to every, day. Pointer looked at the first page, turned another and another, and studied them all, then he handed it to Eliot who did likewise.

"Cipher, eh; and nothing except in cipher!" was Eliot's surprised comment, as he handed the book back to Pointer. He explained that he had seen Dawnay take it out at lunch and run over the leaves. "I can't think why he should make entries only in cipher, but I suppose, these big mining engineers, whose reports mean, everything to the shareholders, can't be too careful. Still it's odd too."

"Why?" Pointer asked.

"Not in keeping with his character, I should have thought," Eliot explained. "Look here Pointer, surely the fact that Ozier was as good as murdered too means that it couldn't have been this Gipsy fellow? Why should he kill Ozier?"

"Suppose Dr. Ozier and Mr. Dawnay were sitting together here," Pointer, asked slowly, as he went on with his examination of the room. "Dr. Ozier is given a sleeping draught to make him drowsy, so that he will go to his room, as he apparently did, to sleep off the effects . . . then Mr. Dawnay is murdered. That might be the doing of Gipsy Joe, mightn't it?"

"You don't think so yourself?" came eagerly from Eliot. "You see," he went on in explanation of his tone, "I would like to help. I can help if it's some inside, or family, or business matter. But, of course, if it's all over and done with—" he looked his regret.

Pointer said nothing. Eliot would not let the silence pass, however, and because he liked him and trusted his discretion, well-tried as it had been in that old case, Pointer finally replied:

"I don't think that whoever tied that Michaelmas daisy up around the club had ever handled raffia before in his life, or tied up plants either. Apparently, Gipsy Joe can garden. Also, I should fancy that he's clever with his hands; men of that kind generally have to be; this man was rather clumsy fingered, or, if not that, then exceedingly unused to any sort of manual work.

"Also, Why should he choose a time when Dr. Ozier seems to have been present?" Pointer asked. "For, if Gipsy Joe, he must have poisoned the doctor in the summer-house before or just after he knocked or hit Dawnay on the head, since the butler says that he doesn't know the house itself at all, and so would know no way of getting to the doctor's rooms unnoticed."

"Weatherall thinks the Gipsy dosed both men's drinks, found that it wasn't strong enough for Mr. Dawnay and so clubbed him," Eliot said.

"Desperate character," murmured Pointer a trifle sardonically, "and so impatient. Why not wait until he

would find Mr. Dawnay alone? Mr. Dawnay so often was
alone in the summer-house."

"Ah!" Eliot said exultantly.

"And what does Weatherall make of the telephone call
putting Mr. Mallinson's appointment forward one hour?"
Pointer asked.

"He agrees that that's odd, but he doesn't seem to
think it counts against Gipsy Joe's vindictiveness," Eliot
said. "But it's the women who're odd, I think."

"Quite so," Pointer agreed promptly. "Why does Mrs.
Dawnay hate the parlourmaid? Why does the girl fear her
mistress, though she's devoted to her? Why does that tall
dark girl—Miss Miller—with the strong character loathe
Mrs. Dawnay; who doesn't seem to spare her a glance?
She and Mr. Sebastian Dawnay might be invisible as far
as Mrs. Dawnay is concerned. The trouble is"—both men
lit cigarettes—"Mrs. Dawnay looks emphatically like one
of those highly-strung, very emotional women who
complicate life for themselves and others by an utter lack
of balance."

"Oh, she is," Eliot said, "for good or ill, where she
herself is concerned, her feelings involved, I don't think
that she can see a matter fairly."

"Quite so," nodded the chief, inspector. "In a woman of
a different type the same face, look, bearing, would mean
something vastly more important. Miss Miller, too, is a
type not easily judged. She, too, is the kind to take offence
easily and not to forget it lightly—easy come but very
hard to go, I judge her temper to be."

"The parlourmaid doesn't strike me as a woman to
make mountains out of molehills," Eliot said
thoughtfully.

"Yet Mrs. Dawnay drew away from her as from a
leper," Pointer said; "Mrs. Dawnay—who hasn't come
near her home to-day after getting off the train as soon as
it had left Liverpool Street. And Miss Miller . . . her air of
complete withdrawal from the house and those in it. Why
was she packing? For she was."

"They're all so certain that Mr. Dawnay hadn't an enemy in the world barring Gipsy Joe," Eliot said disconsolately, after a second's pause. "Do you really think Dr. Ozier was drugged in the summerhouse, and just managed to reach his room before collapsing? And that it was this Gipsy Joe who brained Dawnay and put his cudgel in the flower-bed until he could come back for it after dark?"

"I don't know yet," Pointer said. "But I can tell you this, Eliot; the tops of Dr. Ozier's shoes were much spattered with water. Of course, he may have tried to get to his fitted basin and a drink from the cold water tap when he felt his senses going . . . but there are those washed sherry glasses and the corner basin in the summer-house to consider."

"Definitely so!" came from Eliot. "I quite agree!"

The room had nothing else of interest. They saw that the cudgel had merely been hung on a large hook, and could have been taken down easily enough; though a person seated where Charles Dawnay had been would have seen it done unless he were stooping at the time.

Pointer looked again at the sherry glasses which Weatherall had told them belonged in the dining-room. It was an odd detail that they had been washed and put away; it suggested a knowledge of the corner wash-basin, and yet a certain amount of lack of imagination—unless whoever had done it had no idea that another kind of glass was kept for summer-house use.

There had been no scuffle in the little house, of that Pointer was sure. Dawnay had been sitting with his back to the open door; there was no weapon in the place but the cudgel facing him.

Pointer went back into the house. Clare Dawnay was in her room. Mallinson, Lyall and Sebastian were all sitting over some wine in the smoking-room discussing together the double tragedy. Pointer and Eliot were at once asked to join them.

"We're talking of Colonel Richards and the Islas," Lyall said promptly. "Seems a pretty clear case that! For the fact that both Charles and Dr. Ozier were aimed at speaks for itself—and cuts this Gipsy Joe out, I should say."

"What does it say?" Pointer asked. "In other words, what is the Islas, or what are they?"

"You don't know of the most philanthropic movement of the day?" Mallinson asked with a little laugh. "Why, there's hardly another charity which has been so well praised!"

Pointer knew as much about the syndicate in question as most men, but ignorance was his long suit when investigating a crime. He played it again, and was duly told that there existed a scheme for sending British settlers and their families out to a reclaimed part of Bolivia where land was given away provided it would be cultivated and a house built. A syndicate sent out the settlers, sold the necessary implements and building materials very cheaply, and on large mortgages, and bought the fruits of the land—when forthcoming.

The Reclaimed Islas of Bolivia was the name of the syndicate. Some very big people were on the committee and board of directors. Colonel Richards was the secretary. They claimed to make their profits after the third year in the shape of the productivity of the soil and the good prices fetched by the superior fruit to be garnered from their trees. The syndicate had been in existence some three years, and the government's grants for emigrants were mounting each year. They had a stand at every exhibition showing magnificent fruit, and the Islas shares were quite popular on the Stock Exchange. They did not profess philanthropy, but claimed to be a fruit-growing and marketing board, run on lines which should appeal to every one. Being not far from Lake Titicaca the advertisements made great play about the wonderful air and the good effects of salt on vegetation and man.

Into this comfortable sunshine Dr. Ozier had suddenly thrown a bomb, stating in fiery words that the people sent there were sent to their deaths from snakes and pestilence, famine and fever. He had been out there himself and his words bore the stamp of personal experience.

"Charles was backing him up," Lyall went on—he had done most of the talking, "or he was prepared to do so. The real campaign hasn't started yet. They made sufficient stink for the Islas to call together an extraordinary but very private meeting of the committee last week. They deny every word of Ozier's, and Charles intended to meet this in grand style by Mandarins from the Colonial Office, and the F.O. and heaven knows what other exalted spheres."

Lyall took another glass of wine.

"And you?" Pointer asked. "Were you interested in the matter at all?"

"No, I had some shares in the company, but I sold them as soon as I heard what Ozier had to tell us. Charles held no shares."

"Are you interested, Mr. Mallinson?" Pointer asked.

Mallinson shook his head contemptuously. He didn't go in for untried things, he said, unless it was something which he could send trusty people to investigate for him.

"As for Colonel Richards," Lyall continued, "he put in a thousand to get the post of secretary, and does very well out of it. Too well, according to Ozier."

Pointer asked for a description of the man. Mallinson gave it very well indeed. Lyall, however, said that he had never met the colonel. He only knew the name from the company's reports. He added that the importance of what Dr. Ozier had to say, and had already said, might be gauged from the fact that the shares which had been standing around five pounds for the last two years were now down to three, "And the selling is said to be better than the buying," he added. The question was, was the man whom Mallinson had seen in the morning and who had tried that afternoon to get him to come away from the house—which might have meant putting off the finding of Dawnay's dead body for hours—really Colonel Richards? Mallinson mentioned that his car had been a Rolls.

"You bet that the Islas' secretary would have a Rolls," murmured Lyall. "Know that part of the world at all, Sebastian?"

Sebastian shook his head. He talked very little, and kept in the background.

"As for that extraordinary affair of some one telephoning Dawnay in my name, and getting an appointment at three," Mallinson went on, "that suggests—to me—some one who couldn't have got an interview with Dawnay if he had given his own name, but who, knowing of my appointment, hoped to slip in under its cover. Not a bad scheme. It evidently worked. Of course, Dawnay wouldn't be able to recognise my voice after all this time. The talk this morning doesn't count, that only lasted about three minutes. Nothing would have been easier than for some one to have called himself by my name. Pity I didn't come at three," he murmured, "I particularly wanted to see Dawnay."

"Indeed," Pointer said. "May I ask why?"

"Merely a wish to renew a very pleasant acquaintance," Mallinson said smoothly. He had spoken too quickly. He had no intention whatever of letting the world into the secret of his intended purchase.

"May I ask what you chiefly talked about?" Pointer asked. "The idea is to gather whether there was anything particular that Mr. Dawnay had in view for this afternoon . . . any special pre-occupation. . ."

"He told me about a chap who had been nearly killed under a motor-bus," Mallinson said in the tone of one recollecting with difficulty a barely heeded chat. "We had a word about brakes, and what we each of us thought of the traffic regulations."

"I see," Pointer said. "Were you well known by sight to Mr. Dawnay?"

Mallinson looked puzzled.

"As some one asked in your name for an interview at three o'clock, it's barely possible that there was an idea or an attempt—perhaps a successful one—to impersonate you."

"Good Lord!" said Lyall in a tone of great surprise. Eliot's pulses quickened. Gipsy Joe indeed. Here was much more promising stuff.

"I see," Mallinson nodded, "I see. No, I don't suppose he could remember what I looked like five minutes after we had parted." He repeated again how slight was their acquaintance. "I was the one who recollected him first, when we met at the match-seller's, and had I any idea what I was letting myself in for—" the expression on Mallinson's face finished his sentence for him.

"Did you buy a box of matches?"

"We both did. That's how we met again."

"May I see yours? Were they both of the same kind?"

Puzzled, Mallinson showed a little match-box, coated with white, on which was drawn a black enamel outline of the Mansion House. Dawnay had bought just such a one and dropped it in his pocket he said.

Eliot covertly impressed its appearance on his memory.

"Please don't misunderstand the question," Pointer said; "as you may imagine, it's one that we ask every one, even the closest family relations. Where were you at three this afternoon, Mr. Mallinson?"

"In my office, hard at work."

"Seeing any client, sir?

"No. I might have seen my clerk—but I rather think I had sent him off to serve a notice for a client. . . ." Mallinson rubbed his chin and frowned. "I'm afraid I stayed in and didn't see any one until I left, and I don't think I saw any one then either. I didn't take tea in the office, but stepped into a Maison Lyons near—I don't know if any one saw me there, probably some one did, I often go there—then I came out here by car—drove out myself. It's all very annoying. I might easily have had dozens of people who saw me at three—most annoying." He looked vexed.

"And you, Mr. Lyall?"

"I'm afraid I was in my office having a nap," Lyall said promptly. "Mallinson and I had had lunch together, he had stood me port of a kind you can't leave behind you without a pang, and I slept from about—well—I got back to the office at two, and I wrote one letter . . . nearly . . . then I settled myself comfortably to think it over, and then—something hit my ear with a bang, it was the arm of my chair and the clock was showing half-past three. I finished the letter, wrote a few more, and came out here. My cousin had asked me to call at five for a chat, but I met my fiancée, Miss Dawnay, near the house, and she brought me in at half-past fourish."

"Was the talk with Mr. Dawnay to be about anything in particular, Mr. Lyall?"

"My cousin was thinking of coming in with me in a rather profitable proposition of which I had had the offer—something in the way of minerals, which is my— and his—line, you know. I'm a mining engineer, a small one—and he was a big one."

"You two gentlemen are business friends?" Pointer asked next.

Lyall and Mallinson promptly said that they were.

"A solicitor and a mining engineer are parts of a whole," Lyall added with a grin. "He's the bogey man I threaten the children with. 'Should you not pay attention to this request I shall be compelled to place the matter in the hands of my solicitor,' etc., etc."

"And the hour when you, Mr. Mallinson, met Mr. Dawnay in the City?"

"Big Ben was striking eleven as though it knew it was important to mark the exact time," Mallinson said promptly.

"And you parted from each other?"

"After three minutes, I should say. Say five to be on the safe side. I'm afraid no clock struck the minutes, but it couldn't have been longer. Colonel Richards ought to know," he added significantly.

"And how did the talk end?"

"Oh, Colonel Richards hailed him. He'd been chasing after us."

"Could he have overheard the talk?"

"I doubt it."

"Could he have overheard the time for the appointment?"

"Must have. Why?"

"I wonder if it was he who telephoned in your name?" Lyall said suddenly.

"Or a pal of his," Mallinson suggested.

"Does Mr. Dawnay know the colonel at all well? His voice? His appearance?" Pointer asked.

Lyall could not say with certainty, but since the attitude taken up by Ozier had brought the doctor—with Dawnay behind him—and the Islas Syndicate into direct communication, it seemed unlikely that they had not met on several occasions. "Though as Charles was only behind Ozier, it's possible that he himself barely knew Richards," was the upshot of Lyall's cogitations aloud—for they were hardly more definite than that. If Charles knew of anything shady or tricky, he was like a dog at a rat-hole, even as a kid, eh, Sebastian?"

Sebastian had been sitting remote from the others, silent, his eyes half-closed. He now closed them still further, till they looked, like slits in a mask, and nodded without speaking.

"And you, sir," Pointer turned to him, "where were you this afternoon?"

"Driving a new car," Sebastian replied. "I left some time after lunch. I haven't an earthly of exactly when, and I got back, as you know, just when poor Ozier was being taken away."

"You live here, sir?

"No. I live in South Africa. In Southern Rhodesia."

Pointer asked him how he came to be in England, and was told that Sebastian had only run over to see his people, and the old place, and incidentally make some investments in property in London.

He intended to spend six months in England, and was looking out for a furnished service-flat to suit him. While Charles had been a bachelor so to speak, he had stayed on, but he had intended to move as soon as Mrs. Dawnay got back.

Of him Pointer asked many questions as to Charles Dawney's character and manner. According to Sebastian, Charles had plenty of interests, which meant of course plenty of worries; but he was the kind of man who throve on a fight. "The Islas affair," Sebastian added, "Charles looked on as a delightful chance to show up a set of scoundrels."

As far as he, Sebastian, knew, Charles had not met many of the Islas people personally.

Next came Eliot. He had to explain his visit and his afternoon hours like the rest.

Pointer had laid a notebook down on the table as he came in. He now asked the three to write their addresses and telephone numbers in it.

"And now, another question," Pointer said, drawing out a little black book from his pocket. "This was found in Mr. Dawnay's pocket. It would seem to be his, therefore. It's a pocket-diary, and is full of entries. But every entry is in cipher—a number cipher. Was that his custom?"

"A what?" asked Sebastian.

Pointer explained.

"The entries consisted of numbers, mostly in groups, enclosed in square or round brackets, single, double, and even treble. Some were underscored as well. Some of the figures were double, few higher than 10."

Sebastian shook his head in amazement. "I've seen him make entries often enough. Charles always booked every engagement, however trifling, I should say, but I had no idea. . . . Of course I wouldn't have, but I think I should have noticed a cipher."

Lyall said the same thing. He had turned rather pale, but Sebastian looked merely very wooden.

Mallinson said that Charles had made an entry of his engagement with himself; it had looked like a mere entry, and he had no idea that it was in cipher, but certainly there was nothing impossible in the idea..

Mallinson was allowed to hurry away on that, and the two cousins drifted off together.

Alone with Eliot, Pointer glanced again at the telephone numbers given him the moment before. He believed that none of them was written by the hand that had made those cipher entries in the diary. But the odd thing was that those figures were not in Dawnay's writing either, judging by the many figures scribbled by him over his papers in the summer-house. The entries in the diary suggested a short fat pudgy hand; Dawnay's suggested his own lean, long, thin fingers, and were of a beautiful neatness, made with a fine-pointed nib. These entries were made with a broad one. A fountain pen had been used, but the marks were not in the least such as the fountain pen carried by Dawnay would make. Pointer could not see Mrs. Dawnay at the moment, but he must ask her to settle the point in question as soon as possible.

He walked the little room deep in thought, while Eliot lit a cigarette and tried to evolve a startling theory.

CHAPTER SEVEN

WEATHERALL stepped in to say that Morley, Mrs. Dawnay's maid, who was acting as temporary parlourmaid, was outside, and would very much appreciate a word with the chief inspector.

"I'll see her in a moment," Pointer said promptly. "But first tell me, did Mr. Dawnay ever go to the letter-box wearing the felt slippers that he had on when you and Mr. Mallinson found him in the summer-house?

Weatherall looked profoundly shocked. "Certainly not! Oh, certainly not!"

"Did he send anything out to the box after lunch?

"Nothing whatever, sir."

"Quite sure?"

Weatherall was.

"It's an important point," the chief inspector said gravely.

But the butler knew what he was talking about. Mr. Dawnay had not sent anything out to be posted all that day.

That being clear, Pointer had Morley shown in. She was about forty, sallow, thin, and excitable looking.

"It's just before I leave," she began shrilly, coming up to the two men, "and if it was my last word I couldn't say differently. That bracelet watch that Miss Robina is wearing at this very minute belongs to Mrs. Dawnay. Her husband's last gift to her, and that Miss Robina to wear it! And I'm to be sent to Coventry because I see through her, which is more than any one else does!"

Pointer did not stop her. The woman was white hot. She trembled as she spoke. But she only repeated herself. "That bracelet I saw with my own eyes on Mrs. Dawnay's dressing-table just before—we heard of it. The last act of Mr. Dawnay was to put it there. And now that Miss

Robina to go wearing it. The housemaid saw her take it.
Snatched it up just after she heard Mr. Dawnay was
murdered, and comes down wearing of it, before Mrs.
Dawnay had ever seen it. Oh, clever! But that's her!
Clever!"

Pointer had to stop her and pin her down to facts.
They seemed simple.

At two o'clock she had gone into the Dawnays'
bedroom with some silver articles, and had seen a
jeweller's little black and gold case on the corner of the
toilet table. It had not been there an hour before when
she had taken the silver in question away, so she knew
that Mr. Dawnay must have put it there She had opened
the case and admired the watch inside, with its unusual
scroll work

"Put there by him for his wife," she said again. "Turtle
doves they were until the children fell ill and that Miss
Robina got her chance!"

"In love with Mr. Dawnay?" Pointer asked casually.

"Love!" snorted Morley. "Fat lot that kind knows
about love! Wanted to steal him from Mrs. Dawnay, that's
more like it; not for herself—just to get him from Mrs.
Dawnay. But that's neither here nor there, I—I don't
want to make trouble. And no thanks I'll get for it from
Miss Edie—Mrs. Dawnay, I should say—but that's no
matter. What's past bearing is past bearing. I saw that
watch she's wearing on Mrs. Dawnay's dressing-table,
laid there by the dead master. And Fanny, the under
housemaid, saw her sneaking out with it before the
breath was out of Mr. Dawnay's body. She's always
wanted a watch-bracelet since she lost her own. And
Dora, that's the upper housemaid who helps wait at table,
she saw Mr. Dawnay and Miss Robina choosing that very
watch-bracelet for the mistress. 'Give me the benefit of
your taste, Rob,' says the poor man, little knowing!
Snakes on the hearth, as it were! And Miss Robina she
had a look at the catalogue, and she says 'How much do

you want to pay?' And he says, 'Don't think of the price, just choose the one you think the prettiest on that page.'"

"You're leaving?" Pointer asked when she had finished bubbling over.

Tears came to the woman's eyes, but she blinked them away. "Mrs. Dawnay says she doesn't require a maid any more, and I only took the place of the parlourmaid to help her out when Jones had to go home because of her father."

"But surely you're being dismissed rather abruptly?" Pointer said.

She tossed her bead, a genuine old-fashioned toss.

"That's Mrs. Dawnay's way. She prefers it like that. Always. And I certainly have plenty of good places only waiting for me to go to. Lady Black offered me pounds more than here if I'd only come to her. But I was silly," she wiped her eyes angrily, "I was between-maid years ago with Mrs. Dawnay's mother, Lady Cotterham, and worked my way up to housemaid, and then to being the children's maid, and I never thought Mrs. Dawnay would treat me like this! After all I've done for her! But gratitude—there isn't such a thing." Her lips, twitched.

"I think I must ask Mrs. Dawnay to let you stay on for a few days at any rate," Pointer said thoughtfully; "it would be much better for every one."

"But I don't intend to stay on!" came sharply from Morley. "Treated like dirt! Spoken to as if—" she gulped. "I'm not a spaniel, to be kicked into the corner. And all for trying to do my best! I'm leaving to-night for my mother's. It's not far. You can't keep me." Again that toss of the head. "I haven't done anything wrong. I've nothing to reproach myself with. Being over-anxious isn't a crime!"

"Few enough are!" Pointer said to that. But though she looked as if she would like to hold forth for some time longer, Morley shut her lips—thin, ill-natured lips they were too—and grasping an elbow in each well-kept hand, stood there with her head thrown back, the picture of ill-used virtue.

"When did you last see Mrs. Dawnay this morning?" Pointer asked.

"I haven't seen her to-day," she replied loftily, with her head still more in the air. But her knuckles shone white, as did her nails under all their rose varnish, so tightly did she clasp her elbows. "Not until she came home just now . . ." and with that she left them, swiftly and almost violently.

"Odd effect your last question seemed to have on her," commented Eliot

"It had the same odd effect on Mrs. Dawnay," Pointer said. "Curious. . . ."

He asked for Dora the upper housemaid. A tall, quiet looking girl came in. She made a good impression.

"It's true sir," she said when Pointer asked her the question, "the watch Miss Robina is wearing is the one she and the master chose for Mrs. Dawnay. He handed her a price list from the Empire Goldsmiths while I was waiting at table, and told her he wanted to give Mrs. Dawnay a present of a serviceable little watch so which did she think the prettiest on the page that he had opened it at. She talked them over a bit and finally said which she liked, and Mr. Dawnay, he marked it with a cross. Then he entered something in his little pocket-diary, that was nearly a week ago—and it's the same watch as she s wearing now."

"How do you know?"

"The catalogue was lying on the master's table in the study and I had a look at it. It looks prettier on than in the picture, though."

There had been a number of price lists and tradesmen's catalogues in the study in a wicker tray. Pointer sent for the tray, while he had a word with Fanny the under housemaid.

Fanny told a careful and circumstantial story of seeing Miss Robina rush into the Dawnays' room that afternoon and then slip out again with a little dumpy black and gold case in her hand. The empty case was on

the mantel in Miss Robina's bedroom at the moment—
what it held was on her wrist. Fanny had been in the
bathroom putting out clean towels, The time? She was
able to put it at just after three, as she had then gone off
duty for half an hour to change her uniform. Three to
half-past was allowed her, and she kept it to the minute,
she said.

The importance of the time lay in the fact that if she
were telling the truth, and she struck a very truthful
note, then it looked as if Robina Miller knew very soon
after three that Charles Dawnay would not be alive to see
who got the watch which he had apparently meant for his
wife.

Fanny was thanked and sent back to her work.
"Amazing!" said Eliot. "Absolutely and definitely
amazing!"

Weatherall brought the wicker tray. Pointer found the
catalogue in question, and on a page full of plain gold
wrist-watches they found one at eight pounds marked
with a cross.

Pointer went to the telephone. A moment, and he was
connected with the Empire Goldsmiths Company, and
learnt that Mr. Charles Dawnay, the mining engineer,
had telephoned three days ago, and had had the watch in
question sent to his office in Queen Victoria Street,
paying by cheque. No, he had not dropped any word as to
whom it was for, said the salesman, in answer to a
question. The whole transaction had been of the briefest.
Pointer got the number of the watch, then he hung up.

"Well, Eliot, this surprises you?"

"That Miller girl to have taken a watch that didn't
belong to her? Rather! Not the type at all to sneak things,
one would say." Eliot was quite bewildered. "And to want
to get Dawnay away from his wife! I can't swallow that,
Pointer! That woman—Morley—has jaundice. You can
see it in her eye. Robina Miller and Dawnay are cousins
of sorts; and I assure you the girl talked all lunch time
about nothing but how to have the house all bright and

glorious within for Mrs. Dawnay's return. Nor was there
the vestige of any love-making between the two of them!
Besides, Dawnay was ridiculously in love with his wife!
Ask any one who knew them! A rottener idea I never
came across."

"Yet Morley is the type to hold fast to any idea of hers,
I should say," Pointer said. "As to it's being right, that's
another matter. She's the type to look out for slights and
resent them for herself, or for any one she is fond of.
However . . . I'll ask for another word with Miss Miller."

Robina came in almost at once. Eliot saw that she was
not in the frock that she had worn at lunch, short-sleeved,
open-necked, but in a pleated skirt and silk pullover
whose sleeves came down well over her hands.

Pointer asked her a question or two, and then looked
around him.

"Can you tell me what the time is?" he said. She shook
her head. "Sorry," she murmured. She had not glanced at
her wrist. Pointer motioned her to the window. He
touched her left wrist. "Bend forward, Miss Miller, and
have a look! How far around the house can you see from
here? What is the last bush that you can really
distinguish?"

After a few minutes' talk on what could be seen, and
what could not, he turned back to the table.

"Now, there's one more matter I want to clear up, and
a very important one. The Empire Goldsmiths sold Mr.
Dawnay a wrist-watch some three days ago. I have its
number here. The price was eight pounds. Have you any
idea what has become of it?"

"He gave me a watch as a present," she replied coldly.
"I am wearing it at the moment. It may be the one you
mean." She pushed back her sleeve. Pointer looked at it.

"May I see its number?" he asked.

"Why?" she asked, not making a move to take it off.

"Because we consider it important to verify it." He
held out his hand. Reluctantly she placed the watch in it.

She was very pale. The number of the watch was that given him by the Empire Goldsmiths Company.

Pointer seemed puzzled. "I want to get this quite clear." He did, for he felt that it might lead him to understand what it was that lay behind her manner to Edith Dawnay, and Edith Dawnay's avoidance of her. "The servants heard Mr. Dawnay tell you that he wanted a watch for his wife, and asked you to choose one for her from a price-list." He spoke gravely. "You did so. He marked it, and bought it. I don't understand, frankly, how you claim it as yours."

There was no doubt but that she had gone paler still.

"He asked me to choose one for his wife merely in order to find out which one I liked the best," she said after a second's hesitation "He wanted to surprise me with the gift—as he did. I found it to-day on my dressing-table with a note from him. It was to be a little token of the help I had been in the house."

"May I see the note? "he asked

"I let it drop on the fire," she replied steadily. "So sorry. I never thought that there could be any question of Mrs. Dawnay's claiming this watch as hers!"

The tone of the last words was bitter, and there was an undertone of personal antagonism too.

"When did Mr. Dawnay put it on your dressing-table?"

"I found it there, on going up after lunch. That would be about one-thirty."

"Then how did it come to be on Mrs. Dawnay's dressing-table at two o'clock where it was noticed by the servants?" he asked next. She hesitated. This was a jolt, or both he and Eliot were much mistaken.

"I put it there for her to see on her return," she said finally.

"With Mr. Dawnay's letter?" he asked innocently.

"Of course not! He wrote to me." Her tone was cool; but her eyes were fiery.

"And how did the watch get from her table to your wrist?" he went on.

"It occurred to me that it would look more grateful if I wore it. So I slipped it on just to show my cousin Charles how pleased I was with it."

"When?"

"Oh—when I thought of it! Some time after I had laid it on Mrs. Dawnay's dressing-table—say, around three. I can't be exact about a detail of no importance."

"It's a very unfortunate position," Pointer said slowly, in a tone that signified that he had no more questions to ask. She hesitated, then hurried away looking genuinely perturbed, he thought. As for himself, he stood a moment glancing at the illustration of the watch.

Eliot joined him. "What does the odd little affair mean?" he asked under his breath. "Frankly, I don't feel anything like as confident as I was. Funny! But does it mean anything?"

Pointer shook his head. He had so far no theory about this murder or double murders. Miss Miller did not look like a thief. Yet, but for the merest chance, she might have kept the watch, undetected. Was spite, not theft, the motive here? She could bear spite, this young woman, of that he felt certain. He said as much.

Eliot agreed. "A funny thing happened at lunch," he now said. "One moment she was all gay and cheery, and keen on Mrs. Dawnay's home-coming, and then—biff! Like that! All the fun went out and she sat there pale and furious looking. I haven't an earthly as to what caused it. She was fingering Dawnay's pocket-diary when I noticed it, but as to whether she had looked inside it . . . whether anything had caused it. . . ." He explained how he himself had been occupied. "Ozier commented on it when he came in. Thought it was to do with his being late. Dawnay laughed the notion away, and said it was much more likely that she and Morley had been having a breeze. But I assure you she looked capable of scratching some one's face pretty badly as she jumped up and left us."

"Had you or any one just been talking of Mrs. Dawnay?" Pointer asked.

Eliot could not say for certain. "Better ask Sebastian Dawnay. He seemed to me to feel an interest in the damsel and she, I rather thought, in him."

"Indeed!" Pointer murmured; "and it is precisely towards these two that Mrs. Dawnay's manner is so odd; towards Miss Miller and Sebastian Dawnay, both of whom could have been in the house when her husband was murdered. I take her to be a woman of quite average powers of judgment."

"Well above the average, I should say," Eliot said promptly.

"Then what is at the back of her strange manner?—or rather manners, for she treats each quite differently, and is treated differently in her turn. Miss Miller keeps aloof, with a show of hauteur. . . . That watch-bracelet might help to clear it up."

"As for Sebastian Dawnay," Eliot said, "it rather looks to me as though he had been playing some practical joke on Mrs. Dawnay—he used to love them as a boy—and she is too indignant to notice his existence yet awhile."

"He doesn't look like a joker nowadays," Pointer said, "rather too sardonic for practical jokes, I fancy. She treats him—to my mind—as though she has a horror of him."

"But so she seems to have of Morley!" protested Eliot testily. "Deciphering women's moods must be the devil, and ten to one they're misleading. What she feels to-day she probably won't feel to-morrow."

"She shows a horror of Morley, true," Pointer said slowly, "but it's not for a moment to be compared with her feeling towards Sebastian Dawnay. If she had seen him murder her husband and try to murder Doctor Ozier, I doubt if it could be much deeper. However, the first thing is to try and clear up this watch-bracelet affair. I'll see if she will spare me a minute."

"She's bearing up marvellously," Eliot said in warm appreciation

She is," Pointer agreed, "and it's not easy for her either. Sheer will power is making her do it."

Pointer found that Mrs. Dawnay was still in the little sewing-room at the top of the stairs. He guessed that it was a room into which she had very rarely gone, with which she had had hardly any associations. At the moment she sat writing to her children.

Pointer apologised for disturbing her, but where would he find Mr. Dawnay's pass-book? He had Dawnay's keys in his hand as he spoke. She took him down to the study, and indicated a drawer in a writing table. The papers were to be gone through in the evening with Mr. Baird, the family solicitor.

Pointer found the folded, leather bank-portfolio on top. A glance inside it showed Dawnay to have been a man who kept his expenditure well inside his income. He had his balance sheets sent in weekly. One of the last items related to a cheque to the Empire Goldsmiths. Pointer showed the page to Mrs. Dawnay. Could she explain this, and that, item. Last was the watch. She shook her head.

"A presentation to some one in the firm, I suppose," she said indifferently,

"He hasn't bought anything for you yourself lately? You don't think this could be meant for you?"

Her face contracted. "He told me he wanted me to have something as a thank offering for my return here, but the idea was that we would choose it the first time I could go out with him again."

"One always thinks of a watch as a souvenir of that kind," Pointer said.

"I rather thought of choosing one," she said, and fingered the papers with a sad, forlorn hand.

Pointer was sorry for her. He regretted having to add to her burden of strain, but she might unwittingly hold the key to the riddle of her husband's murder.

"I ask about a watch so insistently because your servants are gossiping about the one which Miss Miller is wearing." He went into details.

"But why come to me?" Mrs. Dawnay asked with a flush on her cheek followed by a deep pallor. "You can rely absolutely on Miss Miller, chief inspector. If she tells you that my husband gave it her as a present, he most assuredly did. We meant to make her some present, of course, before she left us, and to-day was her birthday, as I had quite forgotten." She spoke warmly, but Pointer was certain that the watch was an absolute surprise to her.

"Your maid—Morley, is her name, isn't it—has an animus so strong against Miss Miller that, seeing what has happened here this afternoon, one can but wonder if she knows something vital, something that might link Miss Miller with your husband's death, Mrs. Dawnay."

"Never!" came with force and horror from Edith Dawnay. "Morley is an utter fool, chief inspector. I—I—— oh, I have to fight down the curses I would like to say. I can never forgive her! Never. Never!" Mrs. Dawnay was speaking through clenched teeth, and quivering as she spoke. She made a gesture for silence. "I can't bear much more! But don't pay any attention to that meddlesome fool. Hasn't she done enough mischief?" Fury shone in Edith Dawnay's face. Something implacable and hostile blazed in her eyes. "I could curse the day she came to this house."

"Miss Miller?" Pointer asked as though uncomprehending.

"Morley!" the reply was like a screech. "Morley!" Then Edith Dawnay seemed to catch at her self-control and wrap it round her. She was trembling and very white, but she stood with her lips pressed together and a resolute set to her jaw which told the chief inspector that she would say no more.

Curious tangle here . . . between the new widow and the girl housekeeper. And the maid's venom?

The telephone rang. It was from the Nursing Home. Dr. Ozier appeared to be sinking fast. He was conscious, and it would be as well for any member of his family who could do so, to come at once.

CHAPTER EIGHT

POINTER went upstairs again and tapped at the door of the sewing-room. He knew that Morley had just slipped up with a cup on a tray.

"Who is it?" asked the voice of Mrs. Dawnay.

"I have a message from the Nursing Home to which Dr. Ozier has been taken," Pointer said, and after a second Mrs. Dawnay came out, closing the door behind her, but not before Pointer had caught a glimpse of Morley sobbing convulsively.

"Dr. Ozier—Nursing Home?" Mrs. Dawnay looked quite vague for a moment; her eyes were black caverns in her white young face. Then she made a gesture: "I remember! Miss Dawnay telephoned about him—I've hardly thought of him since. Is he all right again?"

"He's sinking fast, they think," and Pointer went onto repeat the matron's words about notifying any friend of the sick man's. At that her face softened. Tears sprang to her eyes, her lips quivered. She put her hands to her face.

"I must go to him, I'm all he cares for—" she murmured brokenly. "He hasn't any relations. And his friends—I don't know how to reach them. Mr. Dawnay would have known, of course, but I don't."

"How long have you known him, Mrs. Dawnay?"

"We—"

"No, no, you personally—?"

"Oh, ever since we were children. His father and my father were tremendous friends."

She went on to say that as for relations, Dr. Ozier's people were in South Africa, and none of them were closely connected with him. As far as she knew, there was no one who should be notified of his danger.

"My husband dead, my old friend dying—it's a nightmare," she murmured. "I must go to him at once." And she turned back into the room behind her, careless of what the open door showed as she picked up her gloves from a chair. She had her hat still on. Morley now stood by the window casting an apprehensive glance at Mrs. Dawnay, who did not look at her as she closed the door again behind herself and went on down the stairs.

Pointer did not go in the taxi with Mrs. Dawney—her car was down at Cromer and her husband's had just been laid up for an overhaul—but he followed it closely, and it was together that they went into the Nursing Home. She seemed hardly conscious of who passed through the doors with her, who stopped at the Inquiry Bureau, and who was shown into the lift with her, and along a passage to a room where lay a man in a bed with two nurses beside him. A doctor was leaning over the end of the bed. He came forward at once, but Edith Dawnay hurried to the bedside and took one of the hands that lay limply on the coverlet. "Vincent!" she said, clasping it tightly. She knelt beside him. "Don't leave me and the children like this, Vincent!" She spoke pleadingly. She put her arm under his head and turned it towards her. "Look Vincent, it's Edie!"

The doctor murmured approvingly to Pointer. "May make all the difference! He needs rousing. His wife, I suppose–"

But the man on the bed gave a shudder, and turned his head again to the wall. There was no mistaking the action, the willed lack of response.

Edith Dawnay jumped to her feet, gave one look at the man on the bed, and, with a face very nearly as pallid as his own, drew a deep breath and turned to meet the doctor's surprised stare and Pointer's expressionless glance.

"He's dead!" came from the bed behind her, as though in full explanation of everything—in a thick tone as though the man's tongue and lips were stiff.

Pointer stepped to him. The eyes were closed—the mouth drawn into a knot.

The doctor was beside him on the instant "But you're going, to pull through," he said cheerily. "How did, it happen, eh?"

"In the sherry," breathed the man on the bed "Must have been that. I reached my room . . . went down."

"You mean your after-lunch sherry?" Edith Dawnay returned to the bed. She asked the question in a voice of horror.

He did not reply. The doctor felt his pulse. Pointer bent lower. "Dr. Ozier, I'm from New Scotland Yard, hoping to catch the murderer of Mr. Dawnay. Can't you tell me more?"

The eyes opened on an instant. "I don't know more," came a whisper. "We went to the summerhouse . . . had a glass of sherry each. . . . I went back to my room—my work—felt faint—don't know any more." He stopped, exhausted.

"But what was the stuff used?" asked the doctor. "I can't guess. Can you?"

Ozier shook his head and closed his eyes. "Tired," he murmured, "tired." And the shadows showed blue around his lips.

The doctor made a gesture to the two others. The man in bed had had enough. The visit had harmed, not helped, him. Mrs. Dawnay stood a moment with her hands pressed together, staring at Ozier.

Eliot was down below waiting to take her back to the house. Edith Dawnay walked steadily down the stairs and took her seat as though in a dream. He sat opposite her.

"Mrs. Dawnay, can't I help?" he asked in a tone of genuine sympathy. "Can't you think of any one who had a grudge against both Ozier and your husband?" But she kept silence, looking, too spent to speak.

Pointer, after seeing Mrs. Dawnay out of the room, turned to the doctor.

"May I see Dr. Ozier's effects? You've heard, of course, about the death of Mr. Dawnay opposite. Dr. Ozier's drugging may be linked with it—may well have been meant to be still more closely linked."

The doctor said he would have them fetched. There was only one interesting thing among them. From a trousers pocket Pointer drew a box of matches on which was drawn on black enamel an outline in white paint of the Bank of England.

On the under side was a dark stain. . . . Blood? A simple test told him it was; whether human or animal remained to be found out, but as Pointer turned over the matchbox and wrapped it up carefully, he felt that things looked black for Ozier. Even his withdrawal from Mrs. Dawnay was explained if, goaded by her in some way, he had struck down his friend. But every one said that Mrs. Dawnay adored her husband and he her, and her manner of receiving the news of his death bore this out. Apparently she seemed heartbroken. Ozier seemed done with life, and not to want to see her.

And this bloodstained matchbox—one man's matches often got into another man's pockets, but these stains were a different matter . . . recent.

No matchbox in Dawnay's pocket, nor in the summerhouse. . . . That burnt envelope . . . was it intentionally burned? And, if so, by whom?

Pointer arranged for a man from the Yard to act as orderly in Ozier's room, and left, the matchbox in his possession. It looked as though Ozier must have been in the summer-house after the murder of Dawnay. Then how had he been drugged? Why had he gone to his room? Those washed glasses—the spatters of water on his shoe tops. Why his withdrawal from Edith Dawnay's arm? Did he think her unworthy, or did he know himself to be so? Had there been something in the past between them which now loomed horrible and black and treacherous? If ever a woman seemed to have loved her husband wholeheartedly, Pointer would have said Edith Dawnay did.

She did not look to him to be a good actress at all. Hot blooded, yes quick to take offence to imagine it but a woman who would be loyal and true, he thought her. Proud in the best sense of the word as well as its lower. And in every word and look and gesture towards Ozier unmistakable friendly, pity without a touch of passion or of any memory in which passion had ever played a part.

He was just leaving the Nursing Home when he was asked to step to a telephone. The message that came through was from the nearest police station. Gipsy Joe had been found and fetched. He was now waiting for the chief inspector to interview him. The station sergeant reported that the man had no alibi for the hours from two to four.

Pointer found Gipsy Joe to be a big, sly, rather sinister looking man. By the very texture of his thick black hair, by the cut of his heavy jowl, he was a man of strong passions; and by the colour of his eye-balls he was a drinker.

"What's this for? Me being brought here? Has Mrs. Dawnay missed a spoon?" the man asked with a sneer.

"Why do you ask?" came the swift reply from the police superintendent.

"There's no one else to link me with," was the indifferent reply. "I'm no criminal, super. Not a peaceabler man living, as well you know, except where Dawnay is concerned."

"Mr. Dawnay, if you please. And I should warn you that as he's been found murdered, battered to death by your cudgel, anything you say after this will be taken down and may be used in evidence. Now then, I repeat, where were you this afternoon during the hours of from two to four o'clock?"

A curious tigerish look was on Gipsy Joe's face He fairly licked his lips.

"Battered to death with my cudgel," he repeated gloatingly, "and some hold that curses don't work! Depends. As to where I was this afternoon—find out!" He straightened himself, his eyes flashing. "I claim to've been in the room behind my shop." And from that he refused to budge.

He was detained pending further inquiries.

Pointer left on that. The interview had only told him that Gipsy Joe could not be set on one side as having had nothing to do with the crime at Regency Avenue. He hated the dead man, and since he had no alibi, in spite of the drops of water on the tops of Dr. Ozier's shoes and the bloodstained matchbox in his pocket, Gipsy Joe would certainly have to stand among the suspects. But, assuming that Mallinson had told the truth, who then had come to see the dead man at three? Some one who wanted to be sure that his death would be known by four? Possibly the diary, if deciphered, might clear this up—if it was Dawnay's—but was it?

Pointer asked again for Mrs. Dawnay, and put the question to her as to whether her husband ever used a pocket-diary.

Her face quivered. "Always. I gave him one every year. A Business Man's Diary was his favourite. Why?"

"Do you happen to know if he used it as a diary only, or as an engagement book, or as both combined as most of us do?"

"Both together. He always entered every engagement, however trivial, in it, and he jotted down anything important, or salient, that he wanted to remember."

"Supposing he intended to see any one, or do anything, or even post anything important," Pointer went on, "would he be likely to enter such things?"

"Absolutely certain to," she said confidently.

"And the cipher he used? Have you any idea of its key word?"

"Cipher Charles used?" she repeated in bewilderment. "What cipher? He didn't use any cipher. Charles!" She smiled for a fleeting moment.

"Then can you read these entries?" He handed her the book taken from Dawnay's pocket.

She stared at it. "That's not Mr. Dawnay's writing! Nor would he write in cipher," she went on. "Why should he? And look here, next week he had several engagements, every evening in fact—there are only two entries for next week. And my birthday is the week after "—her face quivered but again she bit her lip and went on bravely. "There's no entry there at all. The page is blank."

"Have you his old diaries?" Pointer asked. She shook her head. "His diaries were always destroyed."

Pointer was impressed by Mrs. Dawnay's accent of truth.

"Look at the cover, do you recognise it?" he asked.

"It's the same kind of cover," she agreed. "Yes, it looks like his. But those aren't his entries, so it can't be! And here's another gap. We were both going to several things on this date"—she indicated a blank one—"there's not a single entry here. I saw Charles write them down. And here's one of the children's birthdays—nothing entered. Here's the week he had the flu. This isn't his book at all! Some one has changed it! The—whoever it was who—who—" she could not say the dreadful words "murdered him" and left it at that.

Some one who knew what his notebook looked like," she went on, "and so was able to exchange his for Mr. Dawnay's. Some one who knew that my husband jotted down anything important. . . ." She was speaking through clenched teeth.

The door opened, Sebastian Dawnay came in. He gave the chief inspector a very keen glance as he saw him standing with the little pocket-diary in his hand.

"Do you recognise this at all?" Pointer asked him, holding it out. Eliot, who had followed Sebastian in, came closer. There was something electric in the air.

"A pocket-diary of some one's, isn't it?" Sebastian asked casually.

"It was found in Mr. Dawnay's pocket," Pointer said slowly. "Can you tell me if you ever noticed your cousin using it, or one like it?'

"He wrote down some questions which he was going to ask you—in his diary," came from Edith Dawnay. Her eyes were blazing. She was white to her lips. "Some questions. . . ." She drew a deep breath as though struggling for self-control.

"Did he?" Sebastian spoke in a kindly, sympathetic voice. "Poor, poor, chap! Well, let's have a look at them." He reached out a hand. Pointer laid the little diary in it and watched him keenly. So did Eliot. But above all so did Edith Dawnay, though there was no suspense in her stare, it was only baleful.

"What's this?" Sebastian turned the pages over with a shake of the head. "This isn't Charles's diary!"

"No," Edith said, still eyeing him, "no, it's not."

"Then who's is it?"

"There's a possibility," Pointer said as Mrs. Dawnay did not answer, except by the glitter of her dark eyes and a deep drawn breath almost like a hiss, "that the murderer took Mr. Dawnay's diary for his own, and left this in its place. Or there's a possibility that, knowing the notebook contained some entry which he did not wish read, he managed to substitute this, his own diary, for Mr. Dawnay's, perhaps before the murder. If not before the murder, then immediately after it. Of course, there's a chance too that some quite innocent mix-up has taken place, and that Mr. Dawnay had no idea this book wasn't his own."

"No, no!" came from Sebastian, "1 think he entered something in it at lunch to-day.'"

Edith Dawnay made for the door. "I must be quiet for a while," she said in a low, queer voice, as though her throat were constricted.

Eliot who was nearest, opened the door, and saw her almost totter to the stairs.

"And I watched him jot down something about his wife's home-coming," Sebastian went on in a ruminating tone. "There's an entry for the day in question in cipher, but I saw him write it in, and I'll take my oath it wasn't figures, and it was a lot longer than that one line. I didn't watch him, naturally, but neither did I look away. He added about three lines to a space where he hardly had room for it. And I don't believe consecutive writing would look like figures." He was studying the book. "I know that Charles, as a matter of fact, used what I would call printed characters a lot. For headings, and on business envelopes, and so on but I feel sure that he was writing cursive connected characters when I saw him make that entry. And here's another one—last week I saw him jot down the name of some Amontillado which he wanted to order. He wrote it sideways on the margin. Just the name. Well, where is it? There's no sideways entry on the day in question, nor any day last week. Edie's right. This can't be his diary at all!"

"We found it in his pocket," Pointer said. He too felt sure that there had been a substitution. By whom? Why? The answer seemed easy. Whoever had taken Dawnay's would seem to have hoped that a similar notebook would pass muster without inquiry. Pointer had noticed that there was no name, nor address, nor telephone number, in the book.

Sebastian left them then, to see if possibly he could find his cousin's diary in his bedroom or study, he said.

The butler was rung for.

Weatherall, on being questioned, said he knew for a certainty that Mr. Dawnay had his name, his telephone number, and the size of his hat entered in his diary, as well as the numbers of his cars. He identified the diary at first glance, but when shown the entries he, like the others, was certain, he said, that his master could not have written so swiftly in cipher. He was sure that Mr. Dawnay always wrote his entries in his usual neat, very characteristic writing.

Walter Lyall was questioned. He stared very long at the entries for the day before, and shook his head. "This couldn't be Charles'," he said, "there isn't enough writing in it, cipher or not, for this to be his book."

Robina Miller was sent for. She too turned over the pages of the little book. "That's not Charles'," she said with, certainty. "It's not his writing. And he had something about you, Sebastian, at the end of the space for to-day. I didn't read it, but I saw *Ask Sebastian*, and a couple of closely written lines after it."

"You handled it at lunch to-day," Eliot said in answer to a glance from Pointer, "did you notice whether it was this one that lay on the table, or Dawnay's own?"

She replied, with what looked like perfect composure, that she might have played with it without being at all conscious of what she held in her fingers. Just for a second something flitted across her face, but it was too fugitive an expression to read.

Pointer left them discussing the question, and went to the telephone in Dawnay's study. Here he sent off what sounded like an order for different kinds of typing paper to the Yard. The cipher diary was being despatched at once to the Yard's experts and Pointer was notifying them of its despatch. But he had not much hope of any success.

He went back to where the others still stood talking. Going over to a little table by the window he lifted Mrs. Dawnay's hat to place it on a chair, to make room for his own notebooks. She had tossed her hat down when she looked through her husband's papers with him for the first time. The interest in the diary had drawn her away from that end of the room, and the others still stood in a knot where he had left them. Her hat was a light felt, with its brim rolled into a tricorn shape. As he lifted it, a bead dropped out. Pointer placed the hat carefully in the empty paper basket and carried the whole out of the room. No one noticed him. In the dining-room he inverted the hat over a spread-out newspaper and shook it thoroughly. Three more beads dropped. They were hand-made, and of an unusually intense peacock blue. Stepping through the green velvet curtains drawn across the window bay, he looked up at the pelmet that ran around the french window behind them. It was an early

Edwardian affair with an edging of peacock-blue beads. Pointer had noticed some loose beads lying on the floor boards, and Weatherall had explained that Miss Miller and he had put up the pelmet only that morning—around twelve—but that it would have to come down as soon as possible as it dripped beads all over the place. Looking up at it now, Pointer saw that several of the strings were loose or rotten, and that quite a dozen more beads had fallen. Weatherall had explained about the drawing of the curtains to prevent the sunshine streaming in at just this time of the year. When drawn across the bay, they formed an alcove, with the french windows at the back.

Pointer looked at the beads on the table. He rang for the butler.

"Look here, where's the rest of that bead trimming," he began conversationally. "There's some upstairs, isn't there? It's a question of matching some beads I've found— these on the table."

Weatherall looked at them. "They came from in there, sir. From behind those curtains. Off the floor there. Where did you find them? Not in that summer-house?" Weatherall was excited at his own powers of jumping to conclusions.

"No," Pointer said indifferently, "oh, no, they weren't in the summer-house. You think they came from that pelmet there?"

"Must have, sir. Only strip of its kind in the house. Mrs. Dawnay bought it at a sale near here in the country and sent it to be put up there, and in colour it tones wonderful with the velvet, but it's got to come down, and the sooner the better," he stooped to pick up some more of the freshly fallen beads. "Look, sir!" He opened and shut the french window, and a light shower fell inaudibly. "Every time any one comes in or out that happens."

"I wonder if any one did come in or out at lunch time," Pointer said soberly.

Weatherall stood for a moment thinking. "We always keep it closed—the window, I mean. But there was a draught from that curtain, I noticed. Miss Clare came in that way, and Mr. Sebastian went and shut it. And now I do believe Miss Clare said something about having found it open. Which it never is. There's a straight draught to the door, and the curtains, if there was a strong wind, might blow out as we pass with the dishes in our hands, and wrap round us."

There had been no wind at noon down here, he said. Pointer looked at the windows. When shut, they could not be opened from outside. Yet he now felt sure that Mrs. Dawnay had passed through them some time after the putting up of that pelmet, and had left probably before Clare Dawnay's arrival by that entrance. Probably. . . . No one but Miss Dawnay and Sebastian Dawnay seemed to have stepped behind the velvet hangings. Eliot might be able to settle this point, and it was a very important one. But Weatherall seemed to have no suspicion that Mrs. Dawnay had been to the house that day. Pointer thought this absolutely unfeigned. The butler had nothing to conceal in this tragedy, of that he felt sure. He was attached in an ordinary way to both his employers, and considered that he had a very good post indeed. Why had Mrs. Dawnay come, as she seemed to have come, secretly, and gone as secretly—on a day, perhaps at a time, when her husband had been murdered? Add to that the shudder of the man in the bed, the averted face, the effort, puny though it was, yet showing tremendous determination behind it, to move away from that affectionate arm. . . . Ozier, the friend of the husband, so Pointer was assured, though there were some things . . .

He put the beads away in an envelope and left the room.

CHAPTER NINE

POINTER asked to see Mrs. Dawnay once more. He was shown into her room, where she lay on a couch, her face hidden in the shadows.

"Mrs. Dawnay, we have evidence showing that you returned to this house to-day—probably after twelve. Why did you say you hadn't been back here to-day?"

Even in the shadow her face grew whiter still.

"It's not true! I have not been here!" Her hand trembled and tightened on a cushion beside her. The room was full of pain. It shone in those brilliant eyes, staring half fascinated into his own troubled grave ones.

"There is no possibility of being mistaken," he said slowly, and there was not, after her face and the sight of her eyes. "You came back here—on the day your husband was murdered Mrs. Dawnay. You must see that, however unpleasant, you will have to explain your visit."

"I didn't come here! I wasn't here! I wasn't! I wasn't!" And jumping to her feet, Mrs. Dawnay fairly beat the air, with her clenched hands held high above her head, before she collapsed into a heap on the couch, half fainting.

Pointer could not question her further. She was breaking down, but resolute to say nothing to him. Her fury, wild and passionate, was not directed at himself. Her bared teeth, her clenched hands, her air of helpless agonised fury and resentment were not directed at him. But neither, Pointer thought, were they against fate, impersonal fate. It was an odd scene, like all the others in which Mrs. Dawnay had taken any part to-day, yet she looked to him not at all the kind of woman whom one labels as odd—peculiar—abnormal.

Eliot joined him, and Pointer promptly invited him to dine with him in his rooms. Then he went on to the Yard

where he had the account put before him of a man's very
close shave from being run over by a bus, the only thing
of its kind that had happened in the City that morning. It
had taken place near the Bank of England and was
exactly as described by Mallinson. But—it had taken
place a full hour after the time which he had given for his
talk with the dead man.

Pointer got on the telephone to Mallinson Would he
please come to the Yard as soon as possible.

The solicitor drove round instantly, and Pointer did
not waste any time beating about the bush.

"Mr. Mallinson, are we right in thinking that when
you and Mr. Dawnay first met yesterday, after not having
seen each other for a long time, you talked about an
accident which he had just witnessed?"

"Certainly. Part of the time. Most of the time. Why?"

"Did he go into any details about it?"

"Full of them. As I told you, a man was knocked down
by a bus and all but run over. Dawnay retrieved his hat
and brolly for him—they too had escaped extinction by an
inch or so."

"Where was this?"

"Near the Bank of England. In Queen Victoria Street,
I gathered."

Pointer explained his difficulty about the time.
Mallinson opened his eyes.

"Now how could that have happened? I assure you I'm
not psychic." He was exceedingly vexed with himself. He
had only snatched at the incident as a piece of padding to
fill the gap in as to the real talk—the business talk
between himself and Dawnay.

"How could I have learned about it?" Mallinson mused
aloud, to gain time. "I must have heard of it from some
one else," he said finally and quite easily. "It was from
Lyall. Not being of any importance, I suppose I put the
clock back a bit, or forward, was it? By the way, have you
found Dawnay's own notebook yet?"

"Not yet," Pointer said. "But this accident, Mr. Mallinson. I thought you were so interested in hearing about skids and defective brakes that you were calling at Regency Avenue in the afternoon for the sake of hearing more."

"We talked about skids and brakes all right" Mallinson said calmly, "but evidently what we saw before us was the starting point, not some past accident. You can see enough skids around the Mansion House to satisfy any one!"

Pointer agreed. Mallinson seemed quite at his ease, but it was odd. What had they really talked about? Now Pointer had many friends in responsible positions whom he, acting for the Yard, had helped. He could always tap sources of information which were often sealed to most people. He had; among others, a friend who was a well-known writer for one of the big financial papers, a man who lived by his ear, which he always kept close to the ground of the City, a man with a number of helpers always working for him, bringing him every bit of financial information that came their way. From him, Pointer had learnt that Mallinson was believed to be connected with Lyall in a deal over a Bolivian gold mine said to be one of the many gold mines left sealed by the Jesuits when they were driven from the country, and that Mallinson was reported to be selling the mine in question, or rather the government leases and permits and licence to export the mineral if found, this very week to a couple of keen young financiers. So Mallinson and Lyall had both been interested in Bolivia. . . . And Pointer had heard the City's opinion of all the men concerned. Lyall was a wolf-hound, treacherous and clever. Mallinson was a solicitor bent on making a fortune in the City as quickly as possible; so were the young men to whom he was said to be about to sell the lease. Nothing against any of the lot was known. Charles Dawnay, Pointer learnt, was probably quite familiar with the tract of land in question. He might have asked Mallinson out to his house with a

view to talking over the proposed deal. Lyall was his
kinsman. . . . Dawnay was a man who, according to every
report, hated crooked ways. . . . Walter Lyall might have
been told by him of what he intended to tell Mallinson, or
might have even overheard it. . . . Lyall. . . . Pointer
nodded. It was possible that Lyall had been the man who
sent that faked telephone message setting the hour at
three. Ozier's sole connection with the City seemed to be
his efforts to discredit the Islas group.

"I suggest that it was in connection with Mr. Lyall
that you were going to see Mr. Dawnay," Pointer went on
smoothly, "in connection with his sale to you of the rights
in the Madre de Dios mine, the rights which you were
selling to Wakeley Bros.?"

Mallinson gave a short laugh.

"The inquisition and the Council of Ten, or was it
Nine, have been at work, I see. Well, since you know the
facts I must own up, I suppose. Yes, I did mention the
proposed transaction with his kinsman yesterday, and he
promptly suggested my dropping in at four o'clock to see
him. I went at four—and—the rest you know. I have an
idea, as I said, from the way he glared at me, that
Richards, the Secretary of the Islas, rather fancied that
Dawnay might be also going to have me investigate the
charges against the Islas, act for him and Dr. Ozier. I
rather expected myself that that might be the outcome of
Dawnay's invitation. And a very nice plum it would have
been," Mallinson added regretfully. "Now, chief inspector,
I have laid every card I possess on the table," and
apparently Mallinson had, for no questions brought out
any further information.

At dinner, Pointer and Eliot discussed what could
have happened to Charles Dawnay and Dr. Ozier. There
was nothing else that interested Pointer when he was on
a case but the case, and Eliot was all eagerness to solve
this murder which had taken place while he sat writing
in his room. He told himself that had he only slipped into
the summerhouse on his return, everything might have

been different. It lent a poignancy and urgency to the puzzle.

"I shouldn't wonder if the missing diary might not solve it for us," Pointer said as he stirred his coffee thoughtfully. "And it might be a step towards the solution to read this cipher one."

"I understand that there's no cipher that Room Three couldn't read during the War," Eliot said hopefully, "and I take it that Hendon will be as smart."

Pointer looked amused. "You take a certain simple agreed word or sentence, the National Anthem has often been used, write each letter below your message, count round the alphabet to the letter of the message starting with the letter of the key written below it and jot that number down, and so on. . . . Only a knowledge of the key used can read that kind of a number cipher."

"I thought one went by the frequency of certain vowels E in English and so on. . . ."

"Not in this kind of simple affair. The letter E would be represented by a dozen numbers, depending on which letter of the key word or sentence came below it. The only peculiarity about this diary cipher seems to be the use of square or round brackets, and the underlining or overlining of the numbers. . . . I doubt if it can be read."

"Or the murderer wouldn't have left it, I suppose," Eliot hazarded.

Pointer said nothing.

"I suppose he left his own so as to make you think that it was Dawnay's," Eliot went on, "as every one who knew him knew how much he used his pocket-diary. You don't mind my laying down the law like this, I hope?" he asked with a laugh.

"I like it," Pointer assured him. "I never know when a pearl is going to be dropped before me."

Eliot nearly choked over his coffee; but he went on "Well, it looks, I think, as though the idea had just struck him to take Dawnay's diary off with him, and as he was without any duplicate he left his own, after carefully seeing that there was no name on it, nothing to show whose it was."

"Urn-rn, yes," Pointer conceded, "it's quite definitely, I should say, not in the writing of any member of the household. The figures aren't those of Dr. Ozier—besides every one says he scribbled his calculations down on the first thing to hand, and stowed the bits in his pockets. No one ever saw him use a pocket-diary."

"Though he did use a box of matches!" Eliot said significantly. "It's an odd affair!"

Pointer added to its oddity by telling him about the beads that had dropped from Mrs. Dawnay's hat, and what they stood for.

Eliot listened incredulously. "But—good heavens, did she come back to murder him, or to watch him? I have heard it said that it's just as well he's the model husband he is—or was; that she was frightfully jealous of any one who tried to be extra pleasant to him, any woman that is. Perhaps she had reason to be. It sounds fantastic, but the summer-house would make an ideal rendezvous, and she is uncommonly good at Indian clubs . . . it's not possible, is it, that she—" his raised eyebrows finished the sentence.

"I don't suspect Mrs. Dawnay of any hand whatever in her husband's death . . . intentionally," was Pointer's reply. "But I do suspect that she saw something or started something which fills her with bitter remorse, and sent her off hot-foot to confession and a stay overnight in a convent. Something in which her maid Morley was concerned—she bears her a burning grudge one would say—and Morley knows it and feels thoroughly guilty. That missing diary. . . ." He dropped into a gulf of silence. Eliot hauled him up out of it with a question.

"You think Mrs. Dawnay may know the criminal. That means then, if she's not coming forward, that she daren't? "

"Fear wasn't to be seen in her, face to-day," Pointer said slowly. "Many other emotions. Remorse . . . shame . . . wild regret . . . blind fury at some one . . . but no fear."

"Ah," Eliot considered the puzzle, "intriguing! Knows the criminal. . . . It looks as though she might have been hiding in the alcove behind the drawn curtains. She was in the dining room some time after twelve; As people don't usually hide themselves in empty rooms, you think she listened—or watched something?"

"It suggests itself," Pointer said.

"Prudent as ever!" laughed Eliot. "Well, merely going by guesswork, if we accept it that she was devoted to her husband, it looks as though she feared some danger to him, and was on the alert at the wrong moment, and off duty at the important time—hoodwinked in some way— and I suggest by Morley. Her intense indignation towards the woman—Morley's terror of Mrs. Dawnay—suggests that she was guilty of some mistake, and a terrible one."

Pointer nodded agreement with this last. He too believed that Mrs. Dawnay was not able to forgive the woman, and that the maid, devoted to her mistress, was appalled at the consequences of something that she had done, or not done.

"You were the only stranger at lunch," Pointer said rummatingly, "Lucky that I really feel sure of your character, Eliot, and don't include murder among your possibilities."

Eliot looked appalled. "I say! That's true! I mean I was the only stranger to the household circle. . . . But she didn't need to come home to see me eat. It's much more likely to have been Miss Miller she was watching . . . though, frankly, I should say she was waiting her time. Miss Miller and Sebastian yes, but not Charles Dawnay. Or look here, what about the watch . . . that's an idea! Say she had a notion that Robina Miller might collar it, and slipped in to see if she was wearing it. She wasn't, at lunch. She had short sleeves on, and no bracelets of any kind."

"And the cold animosity of Miss Miller, towards Mrs. Dawnay?" Pointer asked.

Eliot made a gesture of ignorance.

"Amazing that! To one who, like me, had heard her talking about Mrs. Dawnay, and what could be done to turn the house into a flower-show for her return. And Clare Dawnay obviously expected Robina Miller to be all sympathy towards Mrs. Dawnay. . . . Robina didn't seem to feel much."

"And Mrs. Dawnay did not expect her to, apparently," Pointer murmured.

"But to go back to the watching brief of the lady," Eliot went on. "It suggests what, according to you, her manner suggests, that she has a reason to suspect some one in the house. Why doesn't she let you in to the secret? Family pride? For, you know, I believe it's Sebastian Dawnay she's watching."

Pointer had thought so since he first noticed Mrs. Dawnay refusing to look at Sebastian.

"What was he like as a boy?" Pointer asked. "Did you know him well?"

"Not at all well. Supposed to be absolutely without respect for any authority, and addicted to pulling any one's leg. Sort of lad the authorities can bear to see leave. Sebastian Dawnay? What should he bring Mrs. Dawnay home for?" Eliot was speculating aloud—"Unless . . . but that's impossible! She was devoted to her Charles. And as to its being suspicion, not love, that brought her, what could she expect to see . . .? It must have been Miss Miller and the watch!"

"It might be," Pointer rather surprised Eliot by agreeing. "Though she may remember now that Sebastian Dawnay is her husband's heir. Unless there's a posthumous son."

"Any question of that?"

"I don't know yet. I shouldn't be surprised. Mrs. Dawnay was putting the most tremendous brake on herself not to give way. And I think she's a woman who usually shows what she feels. Impulsive, isn't she?"

Eliot thought that she was. "It is part of her real charm. A charm, by the way, which seems to've bowled over that chap Mallinson. He once travelled up with her in a train from Bournemouth, he was telling me, and they chatted together. He didn't learn her name, but he never forgot her. It's only a year ago, by the way, so that's understandable. And now he finds her again as the widow of the man whose murder is discovered by his coming to call on him. It's a funny tangle, even in this funny world."

It was.

"Personally, I'm sorry for him," Eliot said, filling his pipe.

"Why?"

"It's always a pity to find your dream again and, according to what he said, Edith Dawnay has been his dream-lady since that journey. Dreams belong in dreamland, in my experience."

Pointer was only listening with the top layer of his mind.

"You are staying in the house," he said suddenly, "and are a friend of hers. Perhaps you can give her a warning against trying to catch her husband's murderer herself, off her own bat."

"Good Lord, you think . . .? "Eliot asked.

"I shouldn't wonder if that were part of the reason for her silence to me as to any suspicions she has. She has them, and strong ones. Definite ones to, or I'm much mistaken."

"And that was why she came back secretly to the house? She suspected trouble rightly enough. Perhaps suspected the criminal." Eliot was aquiver with interest.

"I don't think she would be so overcome at any mention of her visit in that case," Pointer said slowly, "the visit that she wildly denies. And she's not usually given to remorse, I think. But that's as may be. The point is that she may be going to run into very serious danger, and I want you to make this clear to her. Not that I think that would weigh much with her, though it might just now; but you might also tell her that the amateur hasn't a chance of catching a clever criminal, unless it's a case where the police quite clearly can't work."

Eliot grunted. He did not agree with this last sentence.

"I think she feels quite conscious that she is on dangerous ground," Pointer continued thoughtfully, "rather more so than I should have expected. Her face suggested to me that she was telling herself to be very careful, very cautious—to make no false move. Yet she didn't want help. I don't think Dr. Ozier's peril worried her. Whatever idea of the murderer she has, the fact that Dr. Ozier may also have been aimed at doesn't seem to interest her. In other words a foregone conclusion that both would be in danger?" suggested Eliot.

"Possibly."

"What about the odd efforts of Colonel Richards to gain time?" Eliot asked after a long silence.

Pointer could only say that, in his opinion, since the man was known by name, and lived in a house of his own, he could hardly think him connected with the murder. Time gained might have been valuable to Colonel Richards, was the gist of Pointer's words, but his neck would surely be more so. "It's possible he telephoned, instead of Mallinson—supposing Mallinson to be telling the truth," he added, "and had an interview with Charles. Dawnay, who may have intended to employ Mallinson in some work against the Islas Syndicate. But I can't see how any of the board would dare stage a murder. Mr. Lyall underscores his certainty that it was one of them, or some one sent by them, but business murders—one with such a clear string back to the company—seems too naïve to be likely."

"And you think Gipsy Joe too simple? Suppose the telephone and Colonel Richards to lie outside the crime, connected with the Islas merely, doesn't that leave Gipsy Joe the police favourite?" Eliot asked anxiously.

"That Michaelmas daisy," Pointer reminded him. "It wasn't merely badly tied, it was ignorantly tied."

"Yes, yes, thank heaven!" came warmly from Eliot.

There was a silence.

"And where am I to put Ozier?" Eliot spoke as though he were arranging a shelf.

"Ah," Pointer agreed meaningly, "that's the question! Did he strike down his friend in a fit of fury, and then try to kill himself? Is Mrs. Dawnay at the root of the two things? Mrs. Dawnay who went back to her home and won't acknowledge it? Well,"—Pointer set back on the mantel a Chinese puzzle with which he had been playing—"like these globes, we can turn the various incidents round and round till we're back where we were before, except that we know Mrs. Dawnay probably could have got hold of her husband's diary."

Eliot started. He had not thought of this.

"I say!" he muttered, and again after a pause, "I say!" But as a matter of fact he said nothing more for a long time.

CHAPTER TEN

WHEN Eliot and the chief inspector went off together, Sebastian found Robina in the study, looking at the bookshelves under the eye of a plain-clothes man who sat, ostensibly writing down notes, in the window recess. Sebastian suggested that she should come and dine with him. Robina seemed to hesitate for the fraction of a second. "You can come in a dressing-gown if you like," he cheered her on, "we'll take a quiet corner on purpose. What are you trying to do with those doors?"

"Shut them," she said without any further explanation, and followed by him she walked around to them from the outside and tried to open them, first with a hairpin and then with a penknife. The plain-clothes man, not being able to divide himself into two, had taken up his observation post in the square hall for the moment.

"It can't be done," Robina said finally, "except in books."

"I know. Ever lost a trunk key and tried to open the lock? Or get a new key made?" he asked.

"It soon tells you the difference between theory and practice. But those efforts of yours?"

"Clare said she found the window open at lunch, after she came in this way?"

He nodded without speaking.

"I had already found it open before lunch and shut it," she said meditatively. "Then I found it open again and Morley just slipping out of the room, so I told her that it was to stay shut. Yet Clare found it open? And—well— that's all," she finished curtly.

"What an exciting ending," he scoffed, but his mind was on other things. "Example of the way in which

Morley obeys your orders, I suppose. But come along to dinner, I've a lot of things to talk over with you."

"I rather wanted to find that missing diary," she said evasively.

"Did you? So do I. So do apparently a few other people. I've met Walter Lyall twice taking the books out. Looking for something to read he told me. Clare seemed to be helping him choose."

"But come along and hop into my bus."

Half-way through the meal, he suddenly leant forward. They had gone into a quiet little restaurant off Leicester Square and had the place practically to themselves. "You've eaten nothing, Robin."

"And you've eaten just double nothing!" she said curtly, almost grimly. He raised a speculative eyebrow, but he shot her a very alert look.

"You're taking Charles' death as a grievance, Robin. Now, if Edie does, that's natural. But you've not been wronged by it. Then why look so black?"

She said nothing, but her lips tightened.

"What I want to ask you is this, when did you see Walter Lyall"—he rarely referred to him just by his first name—"this afternoon?"

She shook her head. "I didn't see him at any time."

"And—between ourselves—why were you packing, Robin?"

She was leaning back, in her chair. She sat bolt upright now.

"I got fed up with the house. Morley, and so on—" she said vaguely.

"And me?" he asked.

She shook her head without replying. His hand went out and covered hers on the edge of the table. For an instant, eyes downcast, she sat still, then she withdrew her own fingers and looked at him. She had presented all the aspect of a timid early Victorian damsel, but her expression, her eyes, did not fit the picture—hard, straight, searching. He met them with an almost derisive grin curling his strongly moulded lips, but he said nothing, and she turned away a minute later as the waiter came up.

"Why should Walter take the diary?" she asked, as soon as they, were alone together. "I don't suppose you think he murdered Charles, do you?" This last came scoffingly.

"I'm afraid I don't feel as certain as you seem to be that he didn't," was the slow reply. "I saw him playing with that cudgel the only time I've seen him at the house since my arrival. He was all by himself. Clare was coming on out, and he was evidently waiting for her in the summer-house. He was swinging it this way and that, to get the balance of it right. Besides, psychologically speaking, he's the only one of us capable of having done it."

"He's not!" she said explosively. "He has an awfully pleasant smile."

"And a true wolf's eye," he finished. "Believe me, when you get an eye with that red glint showing at times, you have to do with a man who has something within himself capable of murder, which may take command, quite unexpectedly. I've met the type, and I'm always on my guard with it. And when you get a man capable of murder and add a tremendous inducement—for Charles was all out to stop him from marrying Clare—well —" he finished with a grimace, and chose a cigar with care. She was watching him intently.

"I thought it might have been a frightful accident," she said in a low tense voice. "I mean—sudden anger— great strength—a wild blow." Their eyes met. Something inimical was in the air. He stared at her very long and very hard. She returned the look, but with a difference. Her look was the fiercer of the two, his the more guarded.

"There aren't many men who could have struck such a blow—wildly," he said laconically. His face was sphinx-like: "I don't think that was struck by chance, Robina. That blow was meant to kill."

"Gipsy Joe wouldn't want to take Charles' diary," she said after a pause, as though they had been talking of the man.

"Nor would he want to kill Ozier," he agreed. "I don't suppose he knows him by sight even. I wish it had been the fellow, then it would probably end there. As it is—" he hesitated; he seemed to weigh the advantages of talk or silence. Finally he said, "I think Edith may be in danger next."

"Edith?" Her voice sounded bewildered.

"Say Charles was killed as a first step to securing the fortune—Edith is going to have a baby, isn't she?" he said next.

Robina did not answer.

"I fancy so from something Charles said, and his manner to her. If so, well—she may be in danger now," he went on.

Robina looked amazed and incredulous.

"Look here, Robin," he spoke persuasively "there's obviously something between you, some ill-feeling on both sides perhaps. Forget it, Rob, for the moment, even if you drag it out again afterwards. She wants some one to really watch over her. You would be in an ideal position—if you would only take it."

"I don't agree," she said steadily. "I think the idea is fantastic. About Walter, I mean, and Edith's danger. You know—" she stopped herself.

He waited.

"That he should kill Charles because Charles wouldn't consent to his marrying Clare seems impossible enough. Then you add another motive, and say that he wants Charles' fortune, and so may be going to kill Edith next in case she should have a son. . . . The police won't believe such a tale."

"No, you told the police you saw *Ask Sebastian* in Charles' diary," he replied, and his voice was grating.

"I had to tell them that. Then I've done my duty," came from her.

"Your duty is to help me find that notebook," was the reply.

She said nothing for a moment.

"Walter Lyall will be hotfoot after it," was the next thing he said. "You may be sure of that!"

"I'm not sure of it at all," Robina said quietly. "Why should he care?"

"Because Charles had some idea on hand which would put a spoke in his wheel," Sebastian answered promptly. "I don't know what it was. But he spoke to Ozier and me as though he believed he had him on toast at last! And probably jotted down as much in that diary of his, or it wouldn't be missing, in my opinion. I'm sorry to bring a woman into this, but you're intelligent," he added with a grin that showed that he expected a storm to follow his impudence.

"Yes, I suppose I am," she said slowly, and then added: "Rather a curse, I think. But no, I don't, not really. It's both defensive armour and it's a weapon, isn't it?"

Her words appeared to strike him oddly. A sharp glance—a very guarded smile showed on his face. "Sounds like a crossword clue," he said lightly. "What is both protective armour and a weapon? Intelligence? Is it? Now I should have thought it something swifter—surer; something that could divine, something that had wings to surmount difficulties."

"Aren't you thinking of love?" she asked and there was a faint flush, in her cheek.

"I wonder if Charles was being clever!" she said suddenly. "I mean, if he had himself got hold of that notebook in order to do something with it, having the key of the cipher or intending to have it."

"And because he refused to give it up, he was murdered?" He looked startled "That's a very ingenious idea," he said finally, "quite brainy. I wonder if it's possible."

"Charles would show up any fraud," she went on ruminatingly, "at any cost. He couldn't help himself. No matter what interests were involved. And the best way to find the criminal," she continued, "is to find out what is going on, what scheme is on foot, what there is that Charles would have unmasked, at once. Don't you agree with me?" she asked.

"That sounds like the Islas," he said, "and would explain why Ozier was attacked."

She seemed to hesitate. Then: "Don't let any one know, but I saw Dr. Ozier running as fast as he could run into the house here, from the direction of the summer-house. And he looked ghastly! Ghastly!"

"What time?" he asked.

She made a gesture. "Except in detective novels does any one ever look at the time when they see any one running? I stepped out to ask him what was wrong, but he had got in and was on his way to his own room, taking the stairs three at a time and in a rush—I've never heard anything like it. As if the devil were at his heels. Now, of course, Dr. Ozier wouldn't have hurt Charles—not for all the world. I wondered if he had seen some one—something—"

"More likely that he felt himself going, and wanted to get to his own room and bed," he said slowly. "And you can't put any time to this?"

"Before the alarm was given, of course, but not very long before. I should say about half an hour or less. That would be half-past three—or past the half-hour."

"I say!" He looked startled. "That's tremendously interesting. That means that he couldn't have been drugged in the after-lunch sherry, unless it was slow acting."

She hesitated. She looked as though a struggle were going on within her.

"Well?" he encouraged.

"Again this is only for you, and it's no help, for it doesn't affect the case at all, since the doctor isn't the criminal; but he was working on a narcotic; a drug of some sort, and a secret one. I happen to know it because of the cat. I came on him unexpectedly by the garage last week trying to squirt something down Prince's throat. Prince was arched like a croquet hoop. Dr. Ozier had to own up. He couldn't pretend it was a tonic, for Prince is as fit as a fiddle, so he told me that he was working on something which, as one of its by-products, made what he rather thought was a very wonderful narcotic, and he wanted to try it on Prince as it was absolutely harmless. Prince wouldn't believe it," she added with a quick smile. "He won't look at Dr. Ozier since then. I think Prince thinks he had a very narrow shave from assassination. And of course Dr. Ozier being found like that . . . I should be inclined to think that his being drugged had nothing to do with the murder of Charles, that he was just trying something out on himself, and took too much —but for his face when he dashed into the house. It looked wild and desperate and hunted."

Sebastian whistled.

"You can't use that, for it's only my say-so," she put in hastily, "and if there were any question of his being brought into the case . . . suspected . . . I should deny every word of what I've told you.

"I say! What a precious help you're going to be," he mocked nastily.

"Dr. Ozier's not the murderer!" she snapped, as though her nerves were tense.

"I'm sure of it," he said at once; "just as certain as I am that Walter Lyall is."

"That might mean more, if you didn't hate Walter so. You and Charles—both of you."

"Because we know the kind of man he is, or could be— rotten to the core. But about Ozier . . . we both know . . ." He hesitated, as though weighing speech and silence in a balance.

"What do we both know?" she asked, and again her eyes were hard.

"That Ozier loves Edie," he finished. "Every one who has seen them together knows that."

"And I suppose you'll add that Edith loves Vincent Ozier?" she asked.

"Oh, no!" He gave a laugh. "No, no! It's still more patent that Edie adored Charles and him alone. As he did her."

She gave an assenting nod, assenting and yet offhand. There was a sparkle in her eyes that seemed to catch his attention.

"You look like some untamed thing of the woods at times," he said slowly.

"A red glint in my eye, too?" she mocked

"Something of that kind," he replied unabashed. "At any rate, one who can hate with quite healthy vigour. By, the way, what a noble-looking watch-bracelet!"

Her face changed.

"Charles gave it to me," she said to that, in a low voice. "To-day. He left it in my room. His very last gift. That's why I am wearing it."

It struck Sebastian that there was something odd about her look, manner, and voice, though he could not say what—a suggestion of constraint, a dash of almost resentment.

The dinner was certainly not gay, and putting her into the car he drove her back to Regency Avenue almost in silence. He was not coming in yet, he said, as he stopped for her to get out.

CHAPTER ELEVEN

BY morning Pointer found a sheaf of reports at the Yard. Mallinson came first. His character seemed unimpeachable. The same was true of Charles Dawnay; also of Dr. Ozier. Pointer had sent a man down to Mrs. Dawnay's old home the evening before to make certain inquiries among her own family circle. The man was sent in the guise of a servant, with a package for Dr. Ozier, who couldn't find the right address. A chat in the servants' hall had told him of one new, and perhaps important, fact. Dr. Ozier had been a suitor for the hand of Edith Cotterham. She had chosen Charles Dawnay, very much to her parents' regret. Pointer had rather fancied that something of this sort lay in the past; Mrs. Dawnay had seemed so certain that her presence would be just what Dr. Ozier would most want—Mrs. Dawnay, who Pointer was certain had stood in that curtained bow window some time around noon the day before, but who stoutly denied it.

There came now a fuller report on the autopsy. Quite definitely no traces of any narcotic were to be found in the body, and the idea was further negatived by the state of the pupils. So Charles Dawnay had not drunk any doctored sherry. Had any been poured out for him? Or was Dr. Ozier's condition meant to be a sort of alibi for that young man? There could be no further inquiries put to him for some time—if ever.

The next question that interested Pointer concerned Dawnay's will. The solicitor made no secret of it.

It was still the one made on his marriage, in which Charles Dawnay, with the exception of some trifling legacies, left the interest on his own fortune to his wife until the children, if any, should come of age, when all were to share equally. Charles Dawnay had had an uncle, Sir John Dawnay, whose very considerable fortune had come to him as Sir John's next male kin. Failing a son to Charles Dawnay, it would go on his death to Sebastian Dawnay; and, should he die without a son, to Walter Lyall and his son, or sons. Should all three of Sir John Dawnay's nephews and sons of nephews die without a son to inherit, the fortune was to be divided among certain hospitals.

Pointer had a telephone call from Dawnay's stockbroker, whom he had asked to ring up as early as possible. Pointer wanted to know if the dead man held any shares which would fall on the news of his death. The reply was instant. He did indeed. Certain South American Mining shares in particular were dropping to the limit that morning, since it was known that the mine was a peculiarly difficult one and of the sort which had made Dawnay's name. He had had a method for dealing with crumbling or soggy ground which no other man could equal, which was practically a patent of his; at any rate he had been getting a company together to deal properly with the secret method, and the firm of the stockbroker in question was to have had the handling of it. The news of his death was a great blow.

Had there been any selling the afternoon before, after three o'clock, and before four, Pointer wanted very specially to know.

Yes, there had been some selling, but the shares were of the speculative kind that floated up one day and sagged down another, without any definite rhyme or reason. "It's a sickening year on the Stock Exchange," said the voice at the other end of the wire, "we're used to Bulls and Bears, but it's the Hares of these last years that do the real harm. A shadow sends them racing to cover."

Pointer went on to Dawnay's office. Here, after many other questions, he was again told of the dead man's habit of making notes in his pocket-diary. Here, too, the little book that Pointer produced was identified as Dawnay's—until it was opened. He had no partner, but his two managers scoffed at the notion of his entering things in cipher. They did use a cipher in the office, but it was one which Charles Danay had only been able to use with the greatest difficulty. True, he might have had a private one in which he was very proficient, but they all seemed to think this very unlikely and, until proven, quite incredible.

Pointer, who now had Eliot with him, next went on to the offices, of the Islas, and sent in his card to one of the directors, a man called Gordon.

Gordon was a short, clever-looking Jew, with large, dark, magnetic eyes; he was sitting before a table whose lights and, electric bell pushes might have bewildered a telegraph operator. With all the uncanny skill of his race at reading character he merely glanced at Eliot, and addressed himself to Pointer.

"I hope it's nothing unpleasant that made you ask for an urgent interview," he began.

"It's the murder of Mr. Dawnay," Pointer replied "Mr. Charles Dawnay. Your secretary, a Colonel Richards, seems to have been the last person to see him. I understand he had an interview at three with Mr. Dawnay."

"Had he indeed." Gordon looked pleased to hear of it. "I—we—hoped that Dawnay was coming round to see the lack of all proportion in his friend Dr. Ozier's reports. We don't claim that the Islas is a sanatorium, but we do claim that its a boon to our over-populated country."

"Can we have a word with him?"

Gordon looked most apologetic. "The chap's off again! He feels these attacks on us tremendously. I rather think he's gone out there to make some inquiries himself. On the spot. Incognito. Possibly he promised Dawnay to do this yesterday; if, as you think, he had a talk with Dawnay in the afternoon."

"He met a man on leaving and did his best to dissuade the other from going in to talk to Dawnay; but Mr. Mallinson—it was a Mr. Mallinson whom he met—insisted on going on in, and it was then that he and the butler found Mr. Dawnay—with his head beaten in."

Gordon had turned pale, but he looked as blandly pleased with the world as before.

"What an unhappy coincidence," he murmured. "The colonel is always a bit of a bluffer. I don't think Mr. Dawnay saw him at all. I feel sure he didn't. He always refused to. I think the colonel tried for an interview, was refused, and, knowing that Mr. Mallinson was coming at four, hung around to try to keep him out too. Foolish! But dear Richards—a most charming fellow—is impetuous, we all know."

"But why should he keep any one from finding out that Mr. Dawnay was dead?" Pointer asked. Gordon looked at him in pained surprise.

"You've got it wrong. Colonel Richards happened to mention to me that he overheard Dawnay making an appointment with a solicitor by the name of Mallinson, whom Richards knew slightly by sight. He's been about a bit lately with Dawnay's cousin, Walter Lyall, a dark horse in the City, with none too good a reputation. That's between ourselves. Well, the colonel heard them making an appointment, and jumped to the conclusion, rightly or wrongly, that this Mallinson was going to be asked to act for Dawnay and Ozier in their most mistaken effort to damage the Islas. The colonel wanted to prevent this. Not that we have anything to fear, quite the contrary, but solicitors like to earn big fees by doing all the damage they can, and perhaps the colonel hoped to delay the interview until he could convince Dawnay of the utter baselessness of Dr. Ozier's attacks on us, and has gone off now to find the overwhelming proofs to the contrary. Mind you, chief inspector, I don't know this, but I can imagine that that is the explanation of that very unfortunate attempt on the colonel's part to put off the meeting between Mallinson and Dawnay—supposing it happened. Unless, of course, it was some one impersonating the colonel. The trouble is, he may not know what's happened, and probably won't know for days, and even then may not be able to communicate with you or with me at once."

Gordon looked worried.

They could get nothing more out of him. He professed to be himself certain that Colonel Richards had not been near Dawnay's house, but if he really had been there in person, then Gordon said he was sure that his own explanation would prove to be right in the main.

Pointer and Eliot left the office and made for the Bank of England. It was now the hour around which Dawnay and Mallinson had bought their boxes of matches the morning before. Opposite the new building they saw a man selling matches His tray was a double-decker; in the top tray were matchboxes such as Pointer had found in Dr. Ozier's pocket, such as Mallinson had shown him; below were ordinary boxes. The top ones were priced with a 2d. card, the lower ones a penny. Pointer bought an ornamented one and said that Mr. Dawnay, whose murder was in the papers, had bought a similar one yesterday.

"There ain't no ill-luck sold, with these 'ere boxes," the man said in an aggrieved tone. "Mind you, I don't say you're right and I don't say you're wrong. But what's one man in thirty? Thirty boxes I sold yesterday. . . ."

"Do you remember Mr. Dawnay?" Pointer asked.

"Course I do," was the reply. "Do you remember somethink you've read in the papers from one day to the other? Course you do. Remember some of it for weeks and some for always, eh? Mister Scotland Yard officers—Oh, yes, your picture's in the papers too. Well, faces are my pet newspapers—cost less and amuse you more. I didn't know his name before, but he bought a box all right."

"Any one else buy one at the same time?"

"They did. Smallish bloke. Spoke to this Mr. Dawnay, and says, 'I think we've met somewhere before, haven't we?' and this Mr. Dawnay he says, 'I seem to recollect your face, but, like you, I can't put a name to it,' and they both turns away and stand talking a bit. I didn't hear no names but I heard this Mr. Dawnay, say, 'Cricket week, of course! I remember now and with that they goes off together, friendly-like. . . .'"

"Ever seen any of these gentlemen buy any of your matches?" Pointer showed him portraits of Sebastian and Walter Lyall, among several others. The man shook his head.

After a few more questions, they left him. Apart from confirming the sale of the box of matches to Dawnay, the man had also confirmed Mallinson's account of the meeting.

Pointer turned back. Had the match-seller chanced to see the close shave that a man had had from being run over by a bus the morning before? Regretfully the man said that he must have missed this.

Eliot had to go on to see a friend, and Pointer again made for the Yard.

Meanwhile, early in the morning, Mallinson had sent along a wreath for Dawnay and a little bunch of orchids for Mrs. Dawnay, with a very sympathetic note asking her to command him if there was anything that he could do. Lyall came round to his office to thank him for the flowers. They had arrived just as he, Lyall, was leaving.

"How is she bearing up?" Mallinson asked. "Did I tell you I had met her on a railway journey a year ago, and we had a wonderful talk?

"She's a marvellous woman, Lyall. I don't wonder your cousin was so devoted to her."

"Humph . . ." murmured Lyall with a rising inflection. "Was he? Always? Robina seemed rather a pal of his. However, *nil de mortuis*, of course," and Lyall stopped with an air of being able to say a great deal more if good feeling did not forbid. "By the way, the chief inspector chap seemed very keen on knowing what brought you to Charles' house . . . asked me if I knew why you called yesterday. I said I hadn't the earthliest.

"No reason to drag business into this thing, is there? I mean, it's so plainly the Islas people. Personally I think the police are thundering good chaps and so on . . . but feed them a mass of unrelated facts and of course they get indigestion, eh?"

Mallinson did not reply. He was looking rather hard at Walter.

"Oh, definitely!" he said finally, "but up to a certain point only. I mean—well—unrelated facts, as you say, that have no bearing on the case. Of course . . . other facts—"

There was silence for a moment. Lyall broke it.

"Well, of course, that business of ours is definitely no concern of the police. Charles wanted that piece of ground for himself. . . . However, that's all past. What the police need are present, living—vital things, eh? "

"Oh, definitely," agreed Mallinson again. And his tone sounded relieved. Walter noticed it apparently, for he in his turn stared at him.

"You don't think I had any hand in braining my cousin, do you?" he asked in quite a different voice from any that Mallinson had yet heard from him. There was a hint of menace in it.

Mallinson did not instantly assure the other of the ludicrousness of such a supposition. He said nothing for a painful moment. Then he spoke slowly.

"The fact remains—only between ourselves, of course—that your cousin wanted to warn me of something in connection with that land. Sorry, Lyall, but between ourselves, there's no sense in blinking at that fact."

"A mere chance coincidence. . . ." Lyall was pale. "Good heavens, man, what are you insinuating?" His voice again turned nasty, his eyes had an ugly glint in them.

"Nothing," Mallinson said, quite unperturbed by this change, though it might have given some men pause, for the face looking into his wore an ugly expression. "I wanted to be sure, that's all. Definitely sure."

"Well, you can be!" snapped the other, still in the same hard tone, still with the same narrow, evil-looking eyes. "You know that business was straight. Catch you buying a pig in a poke, Mallinson! Don't you suppose I know how you had it investigated and the samples tested? Very well, then, drop this kind of talk. I don't like it. More, I won't stand it." His eyes bored into the other's.

Mallinson held out his hand. "I'm glad to be assured. Sorry. Let's forget my questions. Once settled it's off the map. Definitely."

Lyall nodded sulkily. He was still angry, it seemed. "And is Ozier? I suppose you think I tried to get him too?" Smouldering anger showed in voice and eye.

"Forget it, Lyall," the other said promptly. "I don't believe in bottling things up. Have it out man to man, that's the best way. I've told you that's finished with. Definitely."

"I suppose you know Richards is missing?" Lyall said meaningly.

"That's why I couldn't get him over the telephone!" Mallinson pushed aside his papers. "Most extraordinary his stopping me going in to see Dawnay—or rather, trying to. Dawnay wanted to hear more about this project of ours, which was why I turned up on time—naturally I didn't tell the police the reason for my call."

"Naturally!" came from Lyall easily. There was a pause.

"I wonder—" Lyall said slowly, "I wonder if Richards thought Charles had asked you down to go through the Islas papers . . . that would put the wind up Richards all right—might have made him act as he did. Now he knows of Charles' murder, he's got the wind up, and no wonder. He'll lie low until everything's cleared up."

"And people won't talk?" scoffed Mallinson "just let him disappear, and reappear at will?"

"Oh, he'll have a good excuse, of course! Started off to see the Islas for himself will be the tale told in the office. Well, what about that mine? Your option expires at twelve, you know, and it's twenty to, now."

Mallinson sat a moment, his lips pressed tightly together.

"I intend to re-sell it this same afternoon, he said finally, slowly, "and I want again your solemn assurance that there is no 'snag' unknown to me? That everything is as you describe it here, in these papers?"

"You have had your own geologist's survey made, and your own tests of the ores," came coldly from Lyall. "'I rather resent your attitude, Mallinson. I am not in the habit of selling pups to my friends."

"Then you give me again a solemn assurance that I can absolutely rely on all these statements?"

"My word of honour," Walter Lyall said magnificently.

Mallinson still hesitated, then he picked up his pen. "Very well. I accept your word." He touched the bell for his head clerk. "If you'll repeat that in front of Sims, my head clerk?" Lyall nodded carelessly. Mallinson signed as the head clerk witnessed the signatures. Mallinson drew his cheque, and the papers were locked away until the afternoon.

CHAPTER TWELVE

EDITH DAWNAY hardly glanced at Mallinson's flowers. There was a room full of similar tokens of sympathy and grief. She, like Robina Miller, had spent the night walking her room. When the mind is violently disturbed, the body asks to share the burden. Edith came down into the hall around ten as she heard Sebastian's step below.

"Sebastian!" It was the first time that she had called him by name, for some time. "An old friend of yours, a Major Hatton-Stroud, has written me such a kind, sympathetic note. It seems that he met Charles in New Zealand once. I've telephoned him that you were staying here, and he's keen on seeing you again."

"I'll look him up at once," Sebastian said promptly.

"I couldn't ask him to lunch," her smile was tormented, "but I asked him to come in this morning and have a talk with you—and me."

"How delightful!" he said, meeting her bright sunken eyes with a smile. "When is he coming?

"At eleven."

"Then I'll just have time to dash out and back."

"Don't be late," she said, with something fierce and exultant in her face.

"Oh, I won't be," he assured her as he passed on out.

Walter Lyall was just going out to his car. He looked at her inquiringly. She caught his glance and hesitated.

"What's wrong with Sebastian?" he aked in a low, confidential voice. "Somehow I've an idea that you and he . . ." he paused.

She hesitated another second, then she turned to him impulsively.

"Ask me about it this afternoon when you come back from your office." She spoke with a flash of her white teeth, which did not in the least suggest her smile—Edith had a charming smile. "I'm glad you're here," she went on in a kinder tone, "it's a comfort. Besides—you should be here. . . Charles' cousin."

"Very distant cousin-in-law; though not, I hope, in affection," he said to that, and considered it a very neat effort. "I'll come back for lunch," he flung over his shoulder.

But she had gone on into one of the rooms.

After his interview with Mallinson, Lyall cashed the cheque that had changed hands at its close, and then hurried back to Regency Avenue. Slipping in at the back to escape the crowd of reporters, he found Edith upstairs in her room standing by a photograph of Charles.

"Well, what about Sebastian?" he asked, with frank curiosity.

"He must have gone to meet him at his club," she said viciously.

"To meet whom? he asked.

She turned her back on him and began to pace up and down the room. A car could be heard going to the garage. It was Sebastian Dawnay who came in a few minutes later.

"Had a breakdown," he said cheerfully, "or rather ran into a refuge. Pretty well bent the bus into right angles. Well, has Hatton-Stroud waited for me, or given me up in disgust? What's the matter?" Edith's face made him ask the question. "Not come at all? I'll ring him up at his club and remind him," he said with apparent ease.

She followed him to the telephone, her face still and tense.

"Not there?" She heard him ask after a preliminary question.

"Probably he's on his way here, after all," he said to Edith, who did not reply. "I'm looking forward tremendously to seeing him," he continued cheerily. She went into one of the rooms, and the telephone rang. Mrs. Dawnay was at it before Sebastian could get to it. "Speaking—speaking!" she said in hurried eagerness. "Mrs. Dawnay speaking," she repeated. There followed a message in a man's voice. Her face went ashen as she listened. "Dead! How horrible!" she said in a choked whisper. "Oh, how horrible! Yes, I sent him a message . Yes, I expected him. . . . No, I don't know him at all well. . . . He was expected here at eleven."

Pointer came out of a room where he and Eliot had been talking to pressmen. Eliot was frankly chagrined. He, too had spent a wakeful night. He had thought that to be inside the ring of a crime, as it were, would give him a great advantage. He could not see that in this case it gave him any.

No one in the house acted like a criminal. He felt sure that the murderer was Ozier, or Sebastian or Walter Lyall, but which one? Thinking back over the impression that each had made on him he would have thought Sebastian the most likely choice, but for what the chief inspector had told him about Ozier's shoes. . . . Those drops of water—and then came the ever-present memory of the beads that had fallen off Mrs. Dawnay's hat. Mrs. Dawnay . . . Ozier, and his signs of horror of her . . . Altogether, it was a very subdued Eliot who accompanied Pointer into the City, and later followed him on out to Regency Avenue. after the talk with Gordon of the Islas. Let the motive of Charles's murder be big business, and Eliot had no mistaken ideas as to his qualifications for dealing with it. He knew nothing of the City, except a general impression that most of the rich men there were crooks, open or concealed. Like Pointer, the sound of Mrs. Dawney's voice, with its poignant accents, had startled him. Both of them hurried to where she stood, white and trembling, almost leaning on the receiver, which she had not yet replaced.

"In any trouble that I can help? "Pointer asked her gently.

She turned to him, something shaken in her look. "He's been killed in a motor accident!" she all but whispered, her eyes dilated.

"Who has?"

"A man who used to know Mr. Sebastian Dawnay—and had met my husband too." She added the last very hastily, Pointer thought. The explanation left much obscure, but she looked as though she had had a real shock as she went up the stairs by herself. They heard her lock the door of her room.

Pointer spoke into the telephone. He asked who it was speaking and learnt that it was from a police mortuary. A car had been found badly damaged on the St. John's Wood road. The driver and only occupant of the car was dead, crushed by the steering wheel. On him were found letters which showed him to be a Major Hatton-Stroud, and there was a note seeming to show that a Mrs. Dawnay had asked him by telephone to call shortly after the time of the accident. By chance, the road at that place had been deserted just then, and no one appeared to have actually seen the accident, but it was evident that there had been a collision with some other car, which had crushed it against the lamp-post. The crash had been heard and had quickly brought a crowd, but the car which had caused the accident had got away. It was described variously as a green sports, a blue saloon, a red tourer and a brown limousine.

"Nothing happened to the major, I hope?" Sebastian Dawnay asked at his elbow. "He was rather by way of being a pal of mine, years ago. Dead? Car smashed." He looked shocked. "What a ghastly way to die," he muttered with what seemed to Robina to be real feeling.

"Did Edith know him?" Clare Dawnay asked, coming down the stairs. "She looks frightful! As though she had had another awful shock."

That was why Pointer was at the telephone. He was seeing the shadow of something that he could not explain.

"She was banking on seeing this chap," Lyall said now, looking at Sebastian curiously, "seemed to want to meet him tremendously—to learn something from him, I gathered."

Pointer hung up. He had a word with one of his men outside the house, and then stood a minute in the garden with Eliot.

"I know him by name," Eliot said, but not why. "Mrs. Dawnay takes his death so to heart."

"Who is he? "Pointer asked.

"Big game hunter and bit of a prospector. As Sebastian Dawnay says, it's a shocking way to end. But as to Mrs. Dawnay being so upset over his death—queer!"

"Very," was Pointer's reply. "And he used to know Mr. Sebastian Dawnay as well."

"He looked genuinely upset too," Eliot said, and Pointer nodded assent.

Sebastian had gone into the dining-room after speaking to Pointer. He found Robina there, altering this and that, though nothing needed alteration.

"You're worried," he said rather sharply. "Oh, I don't mean you're not much more than that, but there is something worrying you too—some doubt plaguing you."

"How do you know that?" she asked.

"By your restlessness. You're waiting for something, or worrying over something. . ."

"Do you think one should tell everything to the police?" she asked after a pause. "Is one bound to do so? I mean, won't one be at rest unless one does?"

He gave her a long, covert look. "Everything? Tall order. I should say no. Don't tell anything until you've thought it over, and talked it over too."

"Yet you're the last man I should call cautious," she almost snapped. Her tone was cross.

"You ask any one and they'll tell you that my reputation in the family is that of a very cautious, long-headed chap."

"Your reputation and you are two very different things," she said.

"What do you want to tell the police so badly?"

She was silent.

"Well?" he asked in a tone of genuine impatience—the tone of a man strung up too tensely.

She did not reply to that. "They won't let me leave, or rather, they think that, as I'm here, I should stay on," she said instead. "The police, I mean."

"You told them you were packing yesterday afternoon, didn't you," he said after a pause.

"I was packing yesterday afternoon," she replied in a level voice "Yes, what about it?"

He hesitated. For once he looked as though not certain of what he wanted to say.

"You've no alibi," he finally remarked.

She stared at him.

"Why should I have? Probably the servants haven't one—any of them. I've no motive either. Charles and I were the best of friends."

"People who haven't an alibi should keep as silent as the grave in my opinion," he said finally, "if they know anything or if they don't But let's hear what you know, and see if it sounds important

"I'm the best judge of that," she replied coolly.

He looked at her from under his beetling brows with those light eyes of his.

"I think I can guess it," he replied.

She shot him a surprised look. "You're a good guesser, I've noticed, but I don't think you can!"

"It's to do with Edith, or with me," he replied steadily.

She started. Her surprised glance told him that it was the former, and at that his face relaxed.

"Better keep it tightly to yourself," he said in a kinder tone. "If it's important, she'll tell. I don't see how anything connected with Edith could be important . . ." he went on in a ruminating manner. "Or was it to do with me?" And there was a cold glitter in his light eyes, menacing and probing.

"With you?" She stared, and her own eyes grew suspicious. "You've spoken more than once since Charles's death as though—" she stopped.

"Yes?" he asked, and his voice had an edge to it.

"As though you thought I suspected you of having had a hand in it," she said, turning quite white, but throwing back her head to meet his stare full on.

They stood so for a second.

"What a charming idea," he said slowly, and the cutting tone brought the blood to her cheeks. "I had no idea you would misunderstand my questions quite so drastically."

"I may have misunderstood them," she said, "but there's something wrong . . . there was before Edith had to rush down to the children. What makes her act as she does to you?"

He shrugged. "What makes her act as she does to you, for that matter," he said carelessly, contemptuously, but his eyes had narrowed.

Her lips parted, her cheeks flushed. She seemed suddenly to have thought of something. But she closed her lips tightly.

He eyed her thoughtfully but she did not speak.

"What is it you know about Edie," he puzzled, "what can it be? Must be about Edie herself, and yet. . . . Look here, why did she give this house a miss yesterday and go to that convent instead? Hopped out of the train at the first stopping place after Liverpool Street. . . . I have a feeling that you know why."

Her eyes, sardonic but intelligent, were on him. But still she did not speak. Yet he felt the effort that silence cost her.

"Oh, you're too close altogether!" he said. "What a wife you'd make for a conspirator or a criminal. Wasted on Leslie altogether."

"You've never met him." She spoke with spirit.

"I believe it's a girl," he retorted. "Leslie is a pretty name for a girl."

Both were silent for a moment, then she said slowly: "Will you answer a question?"

"What is it?" he asked.

"What is it that makes Edith frightened of you?"

"What a damned absurd way of putting things. She's not over fond of me—I'm a Rough Diamond—" he grinned at her wryly, "but frightened?" His eyes looked angry.

At that moment Robina was called away on some household matter. Sebastian poured himself out a stiff whisky and drank it down.

CHAPTER THIRTEEN

AFTER lunch, Pointer went over to the nursing home. He wanted a word with Dr. Ozier if that were at all possible The notebook found on Charles Dawnay had proved, as he felt sure that it would, indecipherable. The Hendon experts told him that it depended, as he had thought, on a key word or sentence.

Pointer had had another look at some of Ozier's figures and he still thought that the probability was against his being the writer of those in the little diary. But it must be certainties not probabilities in detective work

He found the doctors at the Home frankly pessimistic about Ozier, and being so they were willing to let Pointer have a talk with him. Their reasoning seemed to be that Ozier had reached a static stage, when any change would be welcome.

The local police doctor was just leaving.

"Frankly I shouldn't be surprised if it were a suicide attempt," he said to the chief inspector.

"That man doesn't want to live. I asked him if he had taken something himself, intentionally or not, and he said, 'Certainly not,' but he sounded very unconvincing. You do when you're ill and trying to tell a lie. It needs health and go to make a lie live. And as a police surgeon I ought to know!" Dr. Hammond added dryly.

Pointer too thought that the finding of that bloodstained matchbox looked as though Ozier might have taken the drug intentionally. The question, if so, was, had he meant to kill himself; or had he meant to drug himself just enough to be found unconscious, and had miscalculated the dose? He looked impetuous, tremendously keen on anything he cared for, Pointer thought.

Pointer had an evenly balanced mind as he was shown into the room where the man with the blue face lay with closed eyes. Something about him suggested utter weariness of spirit—loneliness too.

Pointer decided to try an experiment—or a test. He had received a telephone message before leaving Regency Avenue, and he now held it open on his knee. "I wonder if you would care to hear the doctor's report on Mr. Dawnay," he said. "He was killed, as we thought, by a blow on the head. No trace of any poison or narcotic was found in the body. In view of your condition the most searching tests were made."

A pair of sunken, but glittering, eyes were fastened on him. From the white lips came a throaty gasp. "What's that? What's that?" demanded the man in bed.

Pointer repeated it slowly and clearly. A convulsion shook the bed. Ozier was weeping as though his heart were breaking. Then he looked up and Pointer saw a changed face. A stone had been lifted; the coffin had been opened and a living man could step out.

"Thank God," he said, "now I . . . But I don't understand. He drank it! I put it in." He stopped. Dazedly a hand went to his face, and was drawn down over it; a sigh came from Ozier. "I would like to talk to you," he said unexpectedly. "It may be madness, but somehow—I feel it might mean sanity instead—at least to me. Mrs. Dawnay then—" Again he stopped. "I can't control my thoughts for a moment, they're all over me. All jumping and barking and frisking at the same time."

He lay quiet a moment evidently trying to "down" his leaping thoughts or call them to order. After a moment he turned around. "I'll tell you everything I know—exactly as I know it. I am at work trying to find a good safe anaesthetic or narcotic. One of the by-products of a certain powder has all the appearance of turning out a rival to scopolamin, with its good effects and none of its drawbacks. It can be used for animals, and incidentally in small doses it is a first-class sleeping powder—at least it has had that result with me. I tried it on Dawnay and he said that he had never had a more sleepless night in his life. I wasn't sure if he was ragging, or, because he didn't believe in soporifics, had self-hypnotised himself into staying awake. I felt that my Somnus powder had not had a fair chance. I gave him a small dose about a week ago in his after-dinner coffee, and learnt next morning that he had slept as usual. I decided to give him a full dose in his after-lunch coffee or sherry, and find out the result for myself. I did so—when was it that he was murdered? Only yesterday? Only yesterday!" Ozier seemed to find difficulty in realising that Dawnay had died only yesterday—"it doesn't take any effect until, two hours afterwards—at the earliest. I put the pellet in his glass of sherry at two. I thought he took it. But, if so, traces would certainly be found. It's a combination of—" he mentioned four drugs which Pointer noted down. "Any of them would leave traces. Two are usual narcotics. Two are not. I knew he had an engagement at three, which could not in any wise be affected by the dose, which does not cloud the mind until the instant of taking effect. At four, I went to hunt him up, and found him—with his head battered in— lying in a pool of blood . . . dead . . . dead some time, half an hour at least, I should say. I saw that Gipsy Joe's cudgel wasn't where it usually hangs, and jumped to the conclusion—I think not unduly hastily, not without warrant—that he had been overcome by the drug after all, and so had fallen an easy prey to Gipsy Joe. God, I—" The face on the bed was convulsed, Dr. Ozier was half sitting, his knees drawn up, his arms flung around them, clutching them as a raft in a sea of horrible memory. "I thought he had taken my stuff and so fallen an easy prey to the murderer! With all his senses about him it seemed to me that Dawnay would be the match of any man. I know that he went over to the door with the glass in his hand and turned around with it empty. I took it for granted he had drunk it. But he said before that he could detect the taste. He had a good palate. And I remember now the grin on his face as he said, 'Come in and look me up later on. I've a chap coming to see me at three and I want my brains about me then; come at four, I shall be alone by then!"

Pointer jotted down the statement and Ozier managed to sign it.

"Did he get out any papers while you were there, in preparation for this interview at three?" Pointer asked when that was done.

"He got out a map of Bolivia, I know," Ozier said. "He turned over some of his mining maps, and said: 'This chap ought to furnish all the information we shall want—' it was a large scale map of Bolivia."

"Are you sure of that?"

"Absolutely."

There was such a map among Dawnay's papers. "Sure of that particular State?"

"My dear man, consider my interest in the Islas of Brazil! Bolivia touches the Islas. They're just over the border in a part of the Matto Grosso."

"Did you make any remark about the map?"

"Hardly. Dawnay's a first-class mining engineer. Important stuff is sent out over his signature. I knew by the look of him that he had something very big on, something that pleased him too. He was humming to himself. . . . I believed that he expected to have the Islas people on toast, and would tell me of their rout later on— after the nap which I thought I had supplied him with."

"And when you went to the summer-house again, doctor, you saw Dawnay with his head battered in? Did you go into the room at all?"

"Why, I touched him! How do you suppose I had any idea how long he had been dead? I touched the back of his hand."

"Did you pick up anything?"

"Nothing whatever".

"We found a matchbox among your things that apparently belonged to Mr. Dawnay."

"Oh!" Ozier s tone sounded genuinely surprised. Then, "Yes, I remember! I picked up a matchbox on which I all but stepped. I did it to gain time," he said slowly, "to gain time before having a good look at Dawnay—after I first caught sight of him—and knew he was dead." There was a long silence.

"And then?" Pointer said gently.

"I don't remember very clearly. I thought of Edith Dawnay—of Dawnay himself, best of pals—handed over by me as I thought to his murderer. I took up the wine glasses, his still had a perceptible odour to it. I suppose he poured out the contents on to the bricks by the door. I washed them both, glad to do something with my hands while thinking—thinking I could see no way out. No way on, either. I decided to take sufficient of a dose myself to end matters. Dawnay dead; Edith removed from me by an unbridgeable abyss—even her friendship would be impossible, knowing what I had done. I could never forgive myself. I went over to my room, and swallowed a boxful of the powder, flung the box on the fire, and felt my senses going at once."

"You saw nothing in the room? We came on a piece of burnt brown paper trodden on by some one."

"I stepped on it," Ozier said promptly.

"Was there anything written on it?"

"Dawnay had used it as a spill. He always lit his cigar with a spill. Yes, I saw one of his printed addresses half burnt away—he always wrote them in printed characters."

Can you recall the letters left? "

"I can. Give me a sheet of paper." He had to have his hand steadied. Then he printed:

HOO   COO
        TOO

"Was the map of Bolivia still on the table?" Pointer asked.

"No, the table was quite bare. But Dawnay always cleared things away when he could. He liked a bare table and would fish out a paper—or pencil—as it was needed and put it away again." Ozier put a period to his sentence by fainting.

He soon came round, and Pointer rang the bell and faced the infuriated nurse. After feeling her patient's pulse, however, she calmed herself. Pointer left him then to gather strength for the next questions and went back to Regency Avenue, where he found Eliot waiting hungrily for him. The writer had found his craft impossible. Real life, not puppets, interested him too much at the moment.

"Any clue? Or did you only 'murder' Ozier for nothing?" he asked eagerly.

"Doctor Ozier's better," Pointer said in a pleased tone. He himself had had his doubts. He quickly went over the interview with Eliot.

"The map?" Eliot repeated, struck by Pointer having mentioned it to Ozier. "So Dawnay evidently expected to have Mallinson act for him, as this Colonel Richards feared."

Pointer did not think that that was the map's only interest, which meant possible importance.

"That Dawnay should have put the map away, in a drawer would seem natural," he explained, "but why tuck it away inside a big folder of South American maps, which in its turn was placed at the bottom of the whole stand for portfolios? Seems rather excessive tidiness on the part of Dawnay.

"The Islas papers are in his safe in the study. There are any amount of mining papers and addenda, and so on, in the summer-house for which he might have wanted the map. The top of his blotter was clean, but there is a faint smear as though blood had fallen on a top sheet, which had been removed, and had faintly soaked through to the sheet below."

"No marks of Hoo Coo Too?" asked Eliot with a faint smile. "Sounds as though the map should have been of China. What do you make of that amazing address?"

"Not necessarily China," Pointer laughed a little. "Think of London . . . suburbs. . . . Too suggests ?

"*Tooting*!" came gleefully from the author. "Then Hoo—?"

"I'll try *Hood* first," Pointer said. "As for *Coo*, I fancy Dr. Ozier may have added one *o* too many. *Too* yes, *Hoo* yes, but probably *Co* would be what he really saw."

"Of course!" Eliot tossed his head with a little snap of self-disapproval. "Hood and Co. of Tooting? Let's try for them."

They found W. Hood and Co., Ltd., 778 Black Street, Tooting. There Pointer and Eliot went at once. They found the number to be an empty shop to let. Inquiries next door told of a jeweller's which had given up business over a year ago. *Hood and Co.* was the name over the door but the last owner of the business was a man of the name of Jones. The neighbours thought that the Joneses had gone back to Cornwall. Pointer and Eliot went to the agents whose signs covered the little window of the empty shop, but they learnt nothing more.

"Now what's the clue?" asked Eliot.

Pointer gave a rueful shake of his head. "I had an idea, a hope, that Mr. Dawnay was posting back a book which had got mixed with his own," he said, "as every one swears that this isn't the right one we hold, and I think they're right, though the figures in the notebook we have share one thing in common with Mr. Dawnay—they were made by a man who was used to jotting down numerals, just as Dawnay's papers show a man used to using figures."

Eliot nodded. He had not thought of that point particularly, but it was true.

"I am trying to think how Mr. Dawnay could have got his notebook mixed with this one of Hood and Co.—Jones—supposing he did," Pointer said, after a silence. "There aren't many ways in which you can do that."

"Possibly in the tube?" queried Eliot

"But a man doesn't put down his pocket-diary like an umbrella beside him in a vacant place in the tube," was Pointer's objection to that.

"Especially a chap who writes all his entries in cipher," agreed Eliot dryly.

Pointer agreed, staring at his shoes. "That's what seems to link the writer—possibly—with a crime. But Hood and Co. of Tooting seems a jump. Yet Hood Co Too seems the only address that fits the words Dr. Ozier said he saw. I wonder? That accident in front of the Bank of England—a man nearly bowled over—his hat, his brolly picked up by Dawnay, Mallinson said. What about Dawnay having picked up what he thought was his own notebook from the pavement, and, finding he had got one too many—this one of Jones'—meant to post it back to its owner? It's a possibility."

"You saw Dawnay turning over the leaves of a notebook which he had pulled from his pocket. It may, have been then that he saw what he had done. There may have been a card in it then, and, granted that the pocket-diary looked just like his own, and that he was being very absorbed in some coming interview—and was possibly a little bemused by that sleeping draught, in spite of Dr. Ozier's ideas to the contrary—he might have posted the wrong one, his own, back by mistake."

"And it would go to the Dead Letter Office?" asked Eliot.

Pointer was not so sure. "The postman would drop it in the shop possibly—part of it is occupied. I doubt if they will remember any bulky envelope, but they may. We shall certainly do our best to find out. Perhaps Lyall can help us. Dawnay talked to him, according to Mallinson, of that accident. Possibly he let drop some clue to him."

Eliot did not reply for a moment. "I'm wondering," he said after a second, "whether there might be anything helpful in that accident in itself. . . . Supposing it was some one who didn't want to be seen in England—I know it sounds like a film, but I'm wondering—I think I'll just ramble around in the City—my brokers have an office quite close. I'll see if I can pick up any seeds . . ." and Eliot hurried off.

When he left him, Pointer had a word with the St. John's Wood police. Nothing more was known about the accident to Major Hatton-Stroud. The car that had caused his death had got away with it, and so conflicting were the reports of it still that there seemed no hope of tracing it. Pointer had another word with the Yard expert sent out to see Sebastian Dawnay's car. Sebastian had telephoned to the local branch of his car makers for a mechanic, and a man had duly presented himself half an hour later, purporting to come from them and showing by the very way he touched the car that he knew his business. His report was now coming in. Phillips could find no touch of dark blue paint on the car—the major's car had been dark blue—let alone blood, but Sebastian Dawnay's car had certainly been in a smash of an unusually thorough character. Signs of lamp-post and refuge were clear enough, and damage to the off side too, but nothing more could be ascertained definitely. Unfortunately his accident had also not been seen. He claimed that it had happened near Harrow, and the damage to a lamp and a refuge there showed that something of the kind had happened on that spot, but, the accident had not been officially witnessed. It would have been possible for any one who had seen the damage to claim that he had had an accident there, in order to account for the condition of his car, and yet to have run down Major Hatton-Stroud—the times and distances would allow of this with a fast car, and Sebastian's was a racer.

Pointer sent in the papers to the proper room to be copied and listed, and went out for a word with Walter Lyall He found that gentleman in his office, looking delighted with himself and life in general, and heard from him the same account of Dawnay's description of the accident that he had given to Mallinson.

CHAPTER FOURTEEN

MALLINSON was considerably surprised to receive a telephone message from Mrs. Dawnay around three o'clock. Would he come and see her? She felt that she would like to talk things over with him professionally.

The solicitor hurried round to her. "Anything I can do for you. Anything!" he said warmly as he was shown into a room where she sat writing some letters She had risen so that the light fell full on her ravaged, pallid face.

"You're very kind," she murmured almost absent-mindedly. She was thinking of what she wanted to say to him.

"Please sit down, Mr. Mallinson I asked you to come for a professional talk. You know all the circumstances of this awful affair, and yet you're not a member of the household, nor are you our family solicitor. I want your help. For I know who killed my husband!"

He stared at her, at her tense figure, her white face, and the menace in her dark eyes

"And who poisoned, or was it drugged, the other man?" He could not think of Ozier's name for the moment.

"And you can add, 'and who's just killed Major Hatton-Stroud,' I'm afraid." She spoke under her breath. "I hoped the major would know at once that he was an impostor and convict him in front of me. But it wasn't to be."

Mallinson was puzzled and looked it. "Who was he"?

"My husband had talked to Vincent Ozier," she said swiftly and with certainty, "and so my husband is dead, and Dr. Ozier all but dying."

He could see her quivering with the effort to keep her self-control from failing away. He could hear her stifled, strangled breath which she would not let turn into sobs. A strong character, he felt sure.

"Of course, the Islas Syndicate," he agreed, but not with much conviction in his voice. Like Pointer, he did not see how any one could really suspect that, or any other committee, of laying so clear a trail back to themselves.

"The Islas?" She stared at him in her turn. "Oh, that!" Her tone of contempt was sufficient answer. "No," she shook her head. "Not business, Mr. Mallinson; much nearer home and harder to deal with than that." She was silent for a moment, then she motioned to him to sit beside her and in a low, tense, voice went on: "That little diary would have put the police straight on the right track—and so it has gone, been destroyed. The murderer—" she stopped and gave a shudder, uncontrollable and violent. Then she said in a still lower tone: "Charles was murdered because he was going to show Sebastian Dawnay up as an impostor. I had asked him to. I distrusted the man from the first. Something about him. . . . I was a bit in love with Sebastian at one time, and perhaps that was why I knew he wouldn't have changed like that. This man you've met, bearing that name, isn't Sebastian Dawnay at all."

Mallinson jumped. A real, definite, clearly to be felt jump. This was an idea! This did suggest a most powerful motive for her husband's murder; and he felt sure that she was not speaking lightly, without inner conviction.

"What makes you think so?" he asked after a little pause. She went into the same details as with her dead husband.

"Mr. Dawnay thought of two proof-positive questions to ask him," she went on, "and there and then he jotted down something in his pocket-diary—yes, the diary that has been taken away. He wouldn't tell me what they were, but he was frightfully pleased with them, and said that if Sebastian could answer them, there was no doubt whatever but that he really was—what he isn't, Mr. Mallinson—and that's genuine.

"When Major Hatton-Stroud wrote me, I thought I had him—the man who calls himself Sebastian, I mean. But he's been killed too—murdered, just as Charles was murdered!"

"Tell your suspicions to the police," he begged. "Believe me, Mrs. Dawnay, I may not be old, but I've had a lot of experience, and I've never known any one keep things from the police in a serious case and not bitterly regret it afterwards."

"But if Charles was right in thinking that the real Sebastian has got himself into difficulties, into prison possibly, and if by any thousandth chance he knows of the impersonation and is abetting it, I might stir up trouble for him too, and—well, I was very fond of Sebastian years ago, for a few weeks. Charles, too, was very proud of his family's record. I must go very warily, but I need counsel. I—I need practical assistance."

He nodded, deep in thought. This was an amazing story. How could he test it?

"I wish you were staying here in the house," she began tentatively, but Mallinson did not see his way to falling in with the suggestion.

"I'm afraid my work prevents my doing that," he said in a regretful voice, "but I shall leave no stone unturned to find out the truth about this. Because, if you're right . . . if you're right—" he drew a deep breath and his eyes sparkled with excitement, "why, there's the murderer! Definitely. But I do beg you—I'd go down on my knees if that would help," he threw in with a faint laugh, "to let me tell the chief inspector. After all, any slight danger of getting the real Sebastian into a difficulty seems to me as nothing compared with helping the police. Of course, I'm a lawyer and perhaps it's natural that I should feel that but it's also just common sense."

She shook her head decidedly. "My husband wouldn't have liked it. Besides, if the real Sebastian has let himself be used by this man, if he's in some tight place which this man assured him he could get him out of if he would let him use his name by impersonating him. . . . Charles believed he hadn't heard from him these last four years because possibly he was in prison—under another name, of course. Some hint of his being there may have actually reached Charles. I.D.B. dealings. . . . When this man turned up, he thought that there had been some mistake. Suppose there's some plan on hand which is outside the law, connected with diamond selling, and that the real Sebastian sent this one home in his stead to work it for him? I daren't go to the police until I know the facts and can warn Sebastian to get from under Mr. Mallinson, I have your word that this is confidential?"

"Of course; you're my client," he said at once, "but I urge you tremendously to take the Yard into your confidence."

But to his great annoyance she would not give way.

"Besides there's the danger to yourself," he went on gravely, "if Dawnay suspects that you think his name is—?"

"Dawson. Captain Dawson. I do," she said.

"We had better call him Sebastian Dawnay just the same for the present," he said cautiously. "If he suspects that you suspect him, Mrs. Dawnay, you might be in grave danger. Whereas if the Yard knew, you would be safe—unless—" he stopped. A thought had struck him. "Did your husband leave a will? I suppose he did?"

"He did. His small private fortune comes to me absolutely, and I have my own marriage settlements, of course. I shall be able to manage quite comfortably with the children. But, if my husband left no son, the fortune his uncle left him for his lifetime was to pass to Sebastian—to this man, if he succeeds in carrying off the position."

"If Mr. Dawnay left no son," Mallinson repeated. "I suppose"—he hesitated—" I suppose?" he repeated questioningly.

"I am expecting another baby—in about six months," she said to that. "Of course my husband's solicitors will be told. If it's a girl, it will make no difference, but if it's a boy—he'll be quite wealthy," she finished.

"But, Mrs. Dawnay," he said again in tones of horror, "think of the danger you run, that being so! Of course, I'm only guessing in the dark, but why else the impersonation?—I mean, it looks as though this man came over here on purpose to do what has been done."

She interrupted him with almost a cry of relief. "I wonder! I wish I could be sure that it wasn't those questions which my husband meant to put to him which were the direct cause of his being killed." She had jumped to her feet, her eyes bright and excited. "But why Dr. Ozier? And why was my husband's diary taken, if so?"

"But, of course, the impersonation must remain unsuspected!" Mallinson said, noting how rattled she was to ask so silly a question. She was not a silly woman in reality, he felt sure.

"Of course!" She made an almost apologetic gesture. "My mind is too shaken to function. Of course! But still, the idea that he came over to get that money . . . that he meant to kill Charles anyway. . . ." She drew a deep breath. "I little thought I should ever be thankful for hoping that would prove to be true," her voice was bitter, but one learns!"

Mallinson did not reply. He was frowning down at his hands.

"What is it? " she asked quickly.

"Are you sure that you can bear me to be quite frank?"

"Quite sure," she replied firmly. "After yesterday's blow, nothing can really hurt me. What is it?"

"You say you were fond of the real Sebastian Dawnay once. . . . I suppose you can easily prove where you were early yesterday afternoon?"

"From four o'clock on, I can. Up till then I did some shopping," her voice came rather indistinctly here, "and then I felt as if I wanted some fresh air and walked in Regent's Park for a while admiring the roses, and sat there a bit. I got to the convent in Kensington by four o'clock, I know."

He sensed that she was not being frank with him.

"Mrs. Dawnay, I do beg you to be quite open," he said urgently. "Really it's most awfully serious, terribly serious. If, as we think, this man who, calls himself Sebastian Dawnay murdered your husband and tried to murder Dr. Ozier, and if you were known to have once been in love with him, don't you see that you ought to be quite frank?"

She nodded her head gravely, but she said nothing.

"For instance, if you were so near as Regent's Park—didn't you come back here at all?"

Her face whitened. She bit her lip. She had made a slip and showed that she realised it. A look of intense suffering crossed her face, but she only shut her lips tighter for a second. Then she leant forward.

"Don't ask me that again, Mr. Mallinson. Ever!" she said in a low voice. "No matter what comes, I shan't answer it. Assume that I was nowhere near the house all day."

"But Mrs. Dawnay—" he began. She silenced him with a gesture so resolute, and so full of some tragedy of the spirit, that he realised that she meant exactly what she said. But he told himself that, given sufficient pressure, she would alter her mind. Let her find out, as she might, that she herself, through that old attachment to the real Sebastian, might be in some danger of being included in the crime. For Mallinson believed that, if cornered, the sham Sebastian, supposing him to be an impersonator, would use that as a weapon to buy silence and his escape.

If he threatened Mrs. Dawnay with bringing her into the case, though but by lies, what could she do but let him go? Whether Mallinson would then continue to keep his promise of secrecy to her was quite another matter. For the present, the first step was to find out whether anything bore out Mrs. Dawnay's idea. If true, it certainly would provide a motive that no one could call weak or flimsy or inadequate. Or rather that was the second step, the first—which could run along with it—was as imperative, and that was to get hold of Dawnay's little pocket-diary with the questions which he had intended putting to Sebastian Where was it? Did this cipher-diary belong to the so-called Sebastian?

"What about Lyall? Does he feel as you do?" he asked.

"He doesn't suspect the truth. He had only met the real Sebastian once, as a little boy. But I was going to speak to him. You see, he may be the real heir. If I don't have a son, and if the real Sebastian is dead—as he may well be—Sir John Dawnay's fortune would come to Walter."

Mallinson had not realised how closely Lyall was connected with the money left to Charles Dawnay.

"As for telling Walter," Mrs. Dawnay went on after a second, "I think he should be told. Will you do it? Tell him all that I have told you. He's awfully nice and kind. I've always liked Walter, in spite of—" she pulled herself up; her tongue was running on just because there, was hardly any mind directing it; her mind was numbed.

"This so-called Sebastian Dawnay was out in his car when the accident happened to Major Hatton-Stroud," she said in muffled tones. "He came back with the car all bent and dented and told some tale of a street refuge. . . . Mr. Mallinson, I'm wondering if this Major Hatton-Stroud's death can by any chance be proved not to have been an accident?

"You certainly ought to go at once to the police or let me go," he said yet again.

"If Major Hatton-Stroud's death wasn't an accident they shall be told. At once," she said.

"I'll hold you to that," he replied gravely. Then there was a pause. "And your husband had no suspicions of the man until you spoke to him yesterday morning?"

"He never dreamt of such a thing. Besides, Charles was young. We hoped to have many more children, a son among them. There seemed no motive. What with his own life, and probably other lives between, even I never thought of Sebastian being impersonated because of that fortune, left Charles in such a dangerous way." She sank into a chair. "I want to go back to my children. It's not fair to the baby that's coming to feel such frightful emotions, such agony of mind, such hate. . . ." She shook slightly and pulled herself together. "I want to go away at once after the inquest and the funeral, leaving it to you to prove the truth."

He saw how tired she was of the struggle to keep at least a semblance of calm, and left her.

His interview with Lyall was an excited one, as Mallinson had known that it would be. It took place in the solicitor's office. Lyall raved aloud at the injustice being done him, even when Mallinson pointed out that as Mrs. Dawnay was going to have another child, the odds were as much against, as for, his getting the fortune.

"And he's taken that notebook," Lyall spluttered when he was coherent, "and destroyed it—the pocket-diary in which Charles had written down the questions he intended to show him up with. The swine!"

"I may be able to help you recover that diary," Mallinson said cautiously.

"How?" snapped Lyall.

"Do I understand that I am to act as your solicitor in this matter?" Mallinson asked.

Lyall thought for a moment.

"I know how sinful your charges are," he muttered. "Will you take it on a percentage basis—if I get the fortune?"

"No," Mallinson said promptly. "I won't. My time's valuable. I'll do anything I can for Mrs. Dawnay—that's different; but between us two, it's purely business. However, I could charge you half fees, inasmuch as Mrs. Dawnay, who has engaged me to act for her, would want all possible facts brought together concerning this man, and concerning the whereabouts of Dawnay's missing diary, as it would be of the greatest help in proving him an impostor."

"It's no longer in existence," said Lyall gloomily.

"I've been thinking it over, and I think there's a good chance of recovering it," was the placid reply.

Lyall opened his eyes.

"How?"

Mallinson's reply was to jingle some coins in his pocket. Lyall looked black, hesitated, and finally agreed to Mallinson's taking on the matter for him professionally on the terms offered. A paper having been signed to that effect, Mallinson became more communicative.

"I have a confession to make," he began. "Strictly between ourselves, I have been guilty of the unspeakable crime of moving a piece of paper from your cousin's drive. It was lying by the gate when I got to the house, just an empty, torn envelope. It had never been sealed up but it was the size to have held a pocket-diary easily. I picked it up, mechanically, read the address in Dawnay's writing, what was left of it, before I tossed it away, and went on to the house. Probably it's still in the shrubbery. You might look when you get home. The name escaped me . . . but the address stuck. I always remember numbers easily—it was 2456, Tooting High Street, and there was a huge blot of ink under the street, which was probably why it was thrown away."

"Why the devil haven't you spoken of this before?" Lyall shouted.

"It slipped my memory," Mallinson said truthfully.

"Oh, you lawyers! Nothing's important that doesn't affect yourselves!" snarled Lyall. "No chance of your having got the number wrong?"

"None whatever," Mallinson said definitely.

He had expected Lyall to be out of his office and down into a car and off, hot-foot, to the address, but Lyall stood a moment quite still, then, smoking a cigarette, strolled to the window, still silent, and stood looking down into the street with unseeing eyes. Mallinson busied himself with some papers

Still Lyall stood at the window, his back to the room. One of Mallinson's clerks came in and only then did Lyall rouse himself from his seemingly deep abstraction and, nodding to Mallinson, walk out of the office and to his own rooms where he sat for quite half an hour drawing squiggles on the blotting paper.

Meanwhile Chief Inspector Pointer had stepped in for another word with Dr. Ozier. Was the doctor quite sure that he had seen *Coo*? not Co. on that paper? Ozier was absolutely certain. The quaintness of the *HOO COO TOO* had struck him forcibly. Another question put to him was whether, during lunch, Dawnay had been wearing the felt slippers which he had on when found dead, or whether he had changed into them afterwards?

Ozier said that Dawnay had a painful heel caused by a shoe which he had worn that morning, and had slipped the felt slippers on when he came up to tell him, Ozier, that it was long past lunch-time. He had left Ozier's door open while he was in his own room changing, and had talked from room to room. He, Pointer, had already learnt from Weatherall that Dawnay had not changed in the summer-house, or had any shoes brought to him there.

Pointer did not stay long. Ozier was getting well swiftly, but his throat was painful.

Pointer was in a brown study as he walked away. *HOO COO TOO, HOO COO TOO*, he repeated over and over to himself like a fakir with a prayer formula. And then he had one of those strokes of luck which are so inexplicable, and yet happen so constantly in connexion with names.

He was on the top of a bus at the moment, and had a long stop at a crossing. His eye rested on a window on a level with him. In large white lettering ran *SCHOOL OF COOKERY*, and below in smaller characters *LICENSED BY THE COUNTY COUNCIL*.

Below was a house agent's sheet of properties. But Pointer did not glance at it. *HOO COO TOO.* What about *SCHOOL OF COOKERY, TOOTING?*

He was off the bus, through the string of cars and on to the pavement in a couple of swift dives. A post office was within sight. He rang up the Yard and learnt in a minute that there was a Cookery School at Tooting. The full address was 2456 Tooting High Street, the proprietor a Miss Gurney.

Pointer took a taxi, and sped to the Yard, left his new find on record, got out a car and sped along to the house in question. He found it to be a corner building over a chemist's shop. Miss Gurney was not only in but was giving a demonstration of how to make a chocolate pudding. Fortunately chocolate pudding does not call for great expertness, and she left it to her assistant, while she answered Pointer's few questions. They wanted to trace a man who had had an accident in the City yesterday morning, he said, whose name was not known, but who had had this address on him—apparently as an address to which his letters or parcels could be forwarded. Miss Gurney absolutely denied the possibility of such a thing. She was a slender, red-haired, freckled woman who looked the last person to be engaged in anything underhand. Pointer persisted in his certainty that the man's mail had been sent here, and asked if she had bought the place recently. This proved the explanation. A Mr. Bonar had had the school before, a School of Cookery for Chefs, he called it. She had had it now about a month. Yes, there was a caretaker who lived in the basement, but she did not think that Mr. Bonar had any of his letters still sent here.

Pointer interviewed the caretaker over a pail of dirty water and a mop. Nice gentleman, Mr. Bonar. And affable! Nothing stuck-up about him. He would stand any lady a drink as soon as not. There weren't many like him about. And because he had always been such a perfect gentleman to her, she, Mrs. Biggs, was keeping anything that came for him, safe and tidy, till he should pop in and fetch it.

Pointer asked her if she would add a pencilled note of his, and, accompanying it by a shilling, in lieu of a drink, watched her waddle to a biscuit tin in a cupboard in the passage. She undid a string, took off the lid, and dropped the slip of paper which had been handed her by Pointer into a completely empty biscuit tin.

"But I thought you said you kept his letters for him," Pointer protested, speaking lightly and casually.

"He's been this noon. Took the tin away just as it was in his car, he did, and I started a fresh one, as I always do."

"Where does he live?" Pointer asked. "I might as well go and see him as leave a message."

Somewhere not far off, she said at once, but she couldn't rightly recall the address. Lavender Hill, was it, or Lavender Grove perhaps. No, Laburnham Grove or something of that kind. Something that made you think of the country. Perhaps one of her children could take a letter round for him? Pointer fished for another coin, but Mrs. Biggs' kids, as she called them, were not on the premises. She only came for the day, seven in the morning to nine in the evening.

There was nothing for it but to leave it at that for the moment, and to try to get on Mr. Bonar's tracks by other method. Pointer left by the side area-door and, crossing the street, caught sight of a car drawn up close to the Cookery School—a car that he knew. And inside sat a man that he knew. Walter Lyall. He was staring at the building from roof to pavement, with a dubious, uncertain air. Then he got out, and Pointer saw him go into the chemist's shop on the ground floor.

If the flies were hunting for the sugar, Pointer decided to leave a lump ready for them. He went into a nearby stationers, and purchased a third diary like the one found in Charles Dawnay' pocket and, therefore, the one which he believed Mr. Bonar had taken away in the tin box. He had in his pocket an envelope similar to the one Dawnay used. It contained the blue beads from Mrs Dawnay's hat.

These he transferred to another paper and, slipping the latest bought little diary into the envelope instead, he addressed it in a capital imitation of Dawnay's printed characters to Mr. Bonar, School of Cookery, 2456 Tooting High Street.

With a burnt match in a quiet tea-shop he manufactured quite a passable imitation of a postmark, and presented himself once more at Mrs. Bigg's, with yet another shilling. Could he drop a letter into Mr. Bonar's tin box?

She led the way, seeing that he evidently wanted to do the dropping himself.

A moment later, and the second shilling changed hands, after which, his lump of sugar safely deposited where it might serve as a decoy, Pointer again left by the side area, this time keeping to the side street until some distance down the road. He watched for some time until finally Lyall came out of the shop and drove off. Then Pointer swung himself into his own car and made for the Yard. Lyall had told him that he had no idea of the whereabouts of Dawnay's diary. If Lyall knew of it, others might.

Last night any one in the house in Regency Avenue might well have felt that they would be closely watched, to-night it was possible that they would be deluded into thinking that the house was no longer under observation.

CHAPTER FIFTEEN

THE result of Walter Lyall's cogitations was shown in a talk that he had with Edith Dawnay not a couple of hours after Mallinson finally left his office. He found her once more hunting for Charles' notebook in all possible and impossible places. Robina too was looking. Even Sebastian Dawnay seemed to have caught the fever.

"It's no use, Walter," Edith said at last, letting him lead her to the shady drawing-room. "The diary isn't here! Of course one knew it, but somehow. . . . At least it was something to do," she added under her breath.

"Listen, Edie, I've learnt a most important thing about that diary, in fact I believe I know where it is. Mallinson told me that when he came here yesterday afternoon he found a torn envelope by the gate which was just about the size to have taken a little diary. It was addressed to somewhere in Tooting High Street—No. 2456 as a matter of fact. It didn't strike him at the time, but Mallinson wonders now whether Charles hadn't picked up some other chap's by mistake, and thinking he was posting it back to him, posted his own by mistake."

"You think Charles was posting it back there, and some one took it out of the envelope? Offered to post it perhaps, and didn't!"

"No, I hadn't thought of that," Lyall said, "I think Charles himself wrote a second envelope when he made a blot on the first. You know his careful way. I think he stuffed the first into his pocket, and it blew out, or dropped out probably when he was on his way to the pillar-box. If I wanted the diary as much as you do, I should have a try in Tooting, before the police learn of it."

"I'll go at once. Will you ring for my—"

"It's not so simple as that," Lyall said pursing his lull, soft red lips "I went there myself as a matter of fact. It's like this: a man called Bonar ran a cookery school or shop, or something like that, at No. 2456; I found out that he had an accident yesterday morning—there's a chemist's shop on the ground floor, and he went in and had a cut on his head treated. Well, the caretaker in the basement keeps all his letters for him, in a tin box. She showed me the box, but she wouldn't let me take it away, or take anything out of it, though I saw the diary in it, mind you."

"Walter!" came in a low thrill from Edith. "Could you be sure?"

"I actually had it in my hand for a second, and I am sure it was—you know Charles way of printing addresses, and his envelopes—that thick yellow paper of his. And then it felt like a diary!"

"And you had to leave it behind!" cried Edith. Her eyes glowed: in that diary she felt sure was something that would condemn Sebastian.

"I had to," Lyall said ruefully; "nor does it matter to me as much as it seems to do to you," he added truthfully.

Lyall wanted the diary because he thought it possible that Charles might have jotted down something to tell Mallinson about the Bolivian mining concession, some query . . . and if Mallinson should ever read it, or get to hear of it, he might demand a return of that money paid for the land.

Misrepresentation of facts might be a nasty weapon. . . . Mallinson would be an unpleasant person to deal with if he once thought that he had been swindled. But Edith Dawnay wanted the diary as a weapon with which to convict her husband's murderer of his crime, or rather crimes.

"I must have it!" Edith started up, her face tense. "Oh, Walter, how could you leave it! I'd have offered the woman anything she wanted for it!"

"She wouldn't take money," Lyall said promptly. "You would only have defeated your own ends. No, I'm afraid that notebook must be stolen—burgled—"

"I wish I could do it!" came in heartfelt tones from Edith.

"I have the key to the side door," said Lyall.

Edith stared at him. "What do you mean?"

"Just that," was the reply. "There was a basement room to let, she told me—I was a manservant out of a job, dressed in my late master's cast-offs, and joy-riding in his car; I told her that I wanted to see Bonar about a job as a waiter.

"She let me the basement room at fifteen shillings a week—in advance. I paid it. I, Henry Smith—got a key on another half-crown's deposit, and here I am—ready to move in to-night. Mrs. Biggs goes home at nine, but I told her I could manage quite nicely without her!" Lyall laughed, well pleased with himself; and Edith could have embraced him.

"I shall go there at ten—better allow some time for the good lady to get off the premises—I'll open the door and wait till you come, then I shall leave. I don't want to be mixed up in anything illegal. I can't afford it. But it's different with you."

"Oh, it is! I don't care what happens to me if I can get that diary."

"I shall open the door at ten sharp, and the rest—will be as you like! I, Henry Smith, know nothing whatever about you, Mrs. Dawnay," and he laughed. Edith Dawnay laughed too, but it was a laugh without merriment.

He left her, and found Sebastian, who was in the billiard-room idly knocking the balls about. Lyall told him—in strictest secrecy—of the discovery made by him that afternoon of the whereabouts of Charles Dawnay's diary. He, Lyall, intended to hang around, he said, and wait for a chance to see this Bonar chap, explain to him that the wrong diary had been posted him, and get it back from him.

Sebastian listened with as much rapt attention as had Edith Dawnay.

"Good idea," he said casually. "In Tooting High Street, you say, a cookery school. What a quaint hiding-place for Charles' diary. Your idea of taking a room there was genius, Walter. I think I'll drop in and have a look round your new apartments to-night. May I?"

"I may be late," Lyall said promptly, "but you can look them over just the same. I shall be out from after ten till about twelve, but I'll leave the door open for you to step in, if you like. There's nothing valuable in the place, and each floor locks its own door."

"Right," said Sebastian heartily, "leave the door unlocked, and I'll blow in and help you hold a housewarming."

"Mrs. Biggs will be there till close on ten, so come after that, or she might guess from our talk that I'm not quite the gentleman's gentleman she thinks me."

"Certainly I will!" Sebastian assured him warmly. "Any time after ten I'll blow along."

Lyall had a drink with him, and left, whistling merrily as he climbed into his car.

Mallinson dropped in at Regency Avenue around half-past six, took a cocktail with Sebastian, who seemed in unusually high spirits, and asked for a word with Edith.

He told Edith that he had started inquiries into the life and present whereabouts of the Captain Dawson mentioned by her as Sebastian Dawnay's friend. He hoped to have important news for her very shortly indeed.

Edith ate very little dinner that night. She had it served to her in the little sewing-room where she had been spending most of her time since her husband's death. Afterwards, as she paced the floor smoking cigarette after cigarette, Robina Miller slipped in.

She went up to the older woman: "Edith, let us forget—bury—that incident." She held out her hand.

Edith Dawnay took it and held it tight, her lips quivering.

"Certainly. I don't need your, and Vincent's, contempt to scourge me still more deeply," she said brokenly.

"Vincent? Dr. Ozier didn't see you! I was the only one who could have! He couldn't possibly have seen you from where he sat. You were out of the window before—"

"It doesn't matter," Edith said quietly, "he must have! He won't talk to me. . . ."

"Why, they telephoned twice for you this afternoon from the Home, Edie, but you were out," Robina said. Edith Dawnay had gone out to get some particular flowers which Charles liked; they were to line his coffin.

"He asked for you eagerly, the nurse told me. Didn't you get the message? I left it on the table for you, twisted in a cocked hat."

Edith glanced at a heap of letters on a table. There was a little paper among them.

"I didn't open anything," she confessed. "But oh, Robina what I felt, as I heard you and him talking so kindly of me, planning such charming surprises for my home-coming, and there I stood eavesdropping! I could have died of shame! That wretched woman!"

"Morley suggested it, I suppose? And opened the window for you to slip in to hear us at our lovemaking?" Robina asked dryly, but her hand held Edith's in a friendly clasp.

Edith Dawnay nodded. "She put a note for me in with some sandwiches, telling me to come and judge for myself. She had hinted—things—before, and I had refused to listen. There was something about you sitting on the arm of Charles' chair of an evening. . . . Oh, Robina, I feel a dog! A dog!" again that quiver of the lips. "To think that owing to that awful woman and my own suspiciousness, my last glimpse of my husband was not as he stood and waved to us at the station, smiling and happy, but as I peered at him from a hiding-place, spying on him. I felt it even as I rushed away, I felt degraded! I went to Confession, I meant to stay at the convent for the night, to try to get back to peace and self-respect. When I

saw your eyes light on me—when Charles was looking
through that pocket-diary—I thought I could have sunk
into the earth for shame!" Edith Dawnay closed her eyes
and looked like sinking to the floor at the mere memory.
"Oh, horrible! Horrible! I shall always have that memory
to carry about with me." She gave a shiver. "And I
thought Vincent had seen me too, and felt as you did—"

"I oughtn't to have taken it as I did," Robina said
contritely, "but I can't help myself, Edie. I'm not generous
by nature, nor easily moved. And—and I did think you
should have known me better! And Charles!" She bit her
lip; she had not come to reproach. "But forgive my side of
it as I do yours, Edie, and I'll wear the watch as from you
too," Robina said, glancing at her wrist. "He wrote on the
slip of paper that went with it that it was a present from
you and from him."

"Was that why you put it in our room?" Edith asked.
"Morley swears she saw it there. I can't make out what
the mix-up was about that watch-bracelet."

"Yes, I didn't want it—after—just then—so I put it in
your room, on your table," Robina said, "in the first flush
of resentment. Then I thought it wasn't fair to Charles to
spoil his present that way, and went and took it again
and put it on; as I say, it is now really a present from
both of you." The two young women kissed each other.

"What makes you look so keyed up," Robina asked
when they were both calmer.

"I know you can keep a secret, Robin, so I'll tell you.
I'm going to burgle a house to-night."

Robina only smiled; whatever the poor little joke was,
she was glad that Edie had something to occupy her mind
with just now.

Edith pushed her out of the room, though with gentle
hands. "Don't stay. I'll look in late tonight and tell you all
about it. No, not now!" Her eyes shone and her cheeks
had something of the glow in them that used to make
Edith Dawnay so handsome a woman.

Robina made her way downstairs and sought out Sebastian. For once he had no bantering talk. He seemed preoccupied, and made the vaguest of replies to her inconsequent chatter, so that she at last fell silent. Then, after an interval, he stretched out a hand and took one of hers.

"Robina, if I asked you to, would you come away with me?"

"For a week-end?" she asked coldly. "Or do you mean would I marry you? You're rather vague."

"Marry me," he said, looking down, "but we might have to run for it first."

"I've told you I'm practically engaged to Leslie," she replied, somewhat breathlessly. "Besides, after what has happened in this house, don't you think it's asking a good deal to suggest running for it, as you call it. Why should you run? Why should I have to?"

He said nothing.

"What were you trying to find last night?" she asked, "hunting among Charles' old papers?"

"An address of an old friend." He spoke heavily. "Of course I didn't find it."

"Is that why you tore up all your own old photographs?" she asked quietly.

He gave her one of his mocking smiles and left her.

At eight o'clock, a man presented himself at the area door of 2456 Tooting High Street and rang the bell. His clothes, boots, hands, cap, and the sack on his back suggested a plumber. To Mrs. Biggs, he said, crossly, "Got to see to two cracked tiles on the roof. From Blackman's. I'll leave this sack of cement here to-night and then me and my mate will bring the tiles and start on it in the morning. Only half an hour's job. Will there be any one here at eight?"

"I'm here at eight myself, more or less. Now wipe your boots first! And don't be long coming down. I wants to be off early to-night."

"And I've got to find which of the blasted tiles has gone cracked," said the man humorously. "I'll shut the door tight when I'm done. I'll see to it, mother."

"Not so much 'mother' young man!" bridled Mrs. Biggs. "How'm I to know you won't forget and leave the door open."

"Now then, you know Blackman's," protested the plumber in injured tones. And Mrs. Biggs did; it was the firm employed by the landlord for all repairs. Besides, as she reflected, there was that young man Mr. Smith, he would be in probably.

So she grudgingly said that she hoped it would be all right, and withdrew into her own room to get ready for a long evening in the bar of the Churchill Arms.

On the top floor, the plumber, Alfred Pointer by name, put down his bag and slipped downstairs again. Very quietly indeed he made his way into the coal hole, and waited patiently until Mrs. Biggs went out, well before her time. He heard some one come in before then, heard Mrs. Biggs speak to him very civilly as Mr. Smith, ask whether he would require breakfast, and if so at what hour. Mr. Smith said he always thought a drop of stout a good way of beginning a hard day, and suggested getting in a couple of bottles of that liquid, one of which, he was good enough to say, Mrs. Biggs might like for herself, the other keep for him until he should shout for it. He would be out late at his waiter's job, and would sleep till noon probably.

Mrs. Biggs left, and then Mr. Smith, whose voice was the voice of Walter Lyall, went into his room and shut his door.

At half-past nine Pointer heard the door open again, and steps—the steps of Lyall—move to the area door, which was then unlocked. Then came the sound of steps in the kitchen, off which the coal-cellar opened. Pointer had wedged the door with a lump of coke on entering. The door was tried twice, then Lyall apparently decided that it was locked and passed on, and Pointer, heard him get into a cupboard on the other side of the kitchen. Then all was quiet, but not for long. The area door was opened and quickly closed. Two pairs of feet could be heard entering. Pointer could see light or darkness through the chink in his door; the beam of a powerful electric torch shone on the wall as some one entered the kitchen. He heard Mallinson speaking.

"Mrs. Dawnay, I do deprecate this way of getting at the diary. Still, I agree that it is important—"

"Where is the cupboard?" she said, interrupting him. "Walter said it was under the stairs at the end of the back passage. Let me have your torch, and please don't stay. You'd better not. I'm sorry you came in with me."

"I couldn't let you come in alone . . . who knows who might be here—I mean, besides Lyall."

"Walter here?" Mrs. Dawnay seemed amazed. "Oh, there's the cupboard—" she dashed away, taking the torch with her. Mallinson had apparently relinquished it. Pointer could hear her opening the cupboard door, wrestling for a moment with the tin lid, and then coming back on the instant.

"It's gone!" she said hoarsely. "The tin is empty except for a letter. You say Walter is here?"

"He's taken a room here under another name, so as to be sure to be able to get that diary. Evidently he has got it." Mallinson said with certainty. "Now, Mrs. Dawnay, I think I had better know nothing about what you are going to do. If I know anything of Lyall, you can buy the diary from him for—say—fifty pounds. Well, good-bye Mrs. Dawnay, I'll leave the torch with you. And the best of luck! By the way, in case Sebastian comes, it might comfort you to know that I shall be just outside, waiting till you come out."

"Sebastian!" her tone was appalled for a moment. Then fiercely: "Sebastian, what makes you think he will come?"

"I shouldn't be surprised," Mallinson said slowly, not replying to her question—"and it might be the best possible thing for us all—if you can get him to incriminate himself. I think I shouldn't let him know that the diary is gone," he added thoughtfully.

"I'll tell him I have it!" came promptly from Edith, who evidently was no believer in half measures. "I'll tell him I've read it, and know why he murdered Charles— and tried for Vincent Ozier, and killed Major Hatton-Stroud."

"I shall be close at hand if you need me. Open the window and I shall come at once, and now good-bye for the moment. And the best of luck!"

He shook her hand warmly, and they could hear him closing the area door softly a moment later.

Left to herself Mrs. Dawnay lit a cigarette, groped for a chair and sat down facing the door. And again there was a very short wait. This time the door was opened. With a snap against the wall of the passage, there was the sound of a firm step and the snick of a torch. The steps turned at once to the passage. Again came the sound of the cupboard door being opened and the slight clatter of the tin box as its lid was pulled off in one tug. Then came a clink, as evidently the box was turned upside down, a pause, presumably while the cupboard was being searched, and then the steps came into the kitchen.

Pointer had enlarged a crack in the door with his knife: and could see Sebastian, illuminated by Mrs. Dawnay's torch, while she in her turn was lit by his.

Sebastian made for the window. "I see there's a blanket to pull across," he said, " I think we might as well draw it and switch on the light." He proceeded to do so, then he wheeled and came towards Edith. She was round the table in an instant. Pointer felt for the wedge of coal and dislodged it noiselessly.

"I want that diary," Sebastian said shortly. "Are you on its track too?"

"No," she replied hardily, "I have it." She had evidently been preparing what she would say. If she told

Sebastian, supposing he came for the diary before Walter Lyall got back, that she had passed on the diary into safe keeping, say, sent it to the police, she might trick the man into giving himself away.

Edith Dawnay was a very plucky woman, and she had determined to do her best to play this terrible fish to the bank, and into the hands that would be waiting.

"I have it, Sebastian Dawnay!" she repeated with a mocking emphasis on the name.

"Why do you use that tone?" he asked sternly.

"You don't expect me to use any other when calling you by that name?" she asked witheringly.

"So that's it, is it," he said quietly, but with an unpleasant quiet. "However, that's not what I'm after. I want that diary, Edith, and I mean to have it."

"Don't dare call me by my first name," she said, "I'm Mrs. Dawnay to you, Captain—" she bit back a name.

Pointer saw that Mrs. Dawnay wanted to tempt Sebastian to some act of violence. He believed that she was quite willing to risk life itself to get him arrested in an attempt at murder. A plucky woman, this. He had opened the door slightly, and now stood ready for a jump.

"I want that diary!" Sebastian repeated in the same low unpleasant tone.

Mrs. Dawnay pulled something from her bag; it was a little pocket diary. She too had evidently brought a duplicate. Pointer wondered how many other copies were being bought up by the inmates of the house in Regency Avenue.

Dawnay's hand shot out. Edith was not quick enough to evade it, and he had the diary twisted from her in a moment, holding her with his other arm thrown round her.

"I think I'll wait for dear Walter before leaving," he said through his teeth, "and meanwhile, Mrs. Dawnay, I'm sorry, but I think a cupboard the best place for you until I can take you safely home."

Still holding her easily with his one arm, he stepped towards the cupboard where Lyall had hidden himself.

Sebastian Dawnay, to continue to give him that name, whether his or not, flung the cupboard door open and bundled Edith Dawnay in, without casting a glance into its farther end. It was a deep one running well to the left of its door. She had not uttered a sound. Now she screamed—once. Pointer was at the cupboard in one leap and had her out. There was a red mark on her throat.

"Don't scream, Edie!" came from Lyall, who followed her out. "I hope I haven't hurt you, but don't scream. We want to settle this by ourselves without the neighbourhood taking a hand. Chief inspector, I'm glad you're here!"

"So am I," came Mallinson's quiet voice from the doorway.

"Mrs. Dawnay, do sit down; I hope you haven't been roughly handled—a dangerous game to play, that of the tethered goat." Pointer got her a glass of water. She gulped it down and thanked him.

"I want you to arrest that man"—she pointed to Sebastian. "And Walter, I want the diary from you that Charles sent away by mistake—his own diary. You have it, we know."

"Then you know more than I do," he retorted savagely. He looked in a very evil temper.

CHAPTER SIXTEEN

"SUPPOSE you hand the missing diary to the chief inspector, Lyall, and let him deal with it—and the whole situation Mallinson said. "I presume you intend to charge this man with assault, Mrs. Dawnay?" He glanced at Sebastian Dawnay, who showed his teeth at him.

"Charge Lyall, you mean," he retorted, "he tried to strangle her. I only bundled her into the cupboard."

"And you are only an impostor," came from Lyall, who was trembling with passion, "trying to pass yourself off as my cousin's cousin and heir. You, who murdered him because he saw through you! Chief inspector, I ask you, we all ask you, to arrest this man for the murder of Charles Dawnay and that poor chap Major Hatton-Stroud, and the attempted murder of Dr. Ozier."

"Unmasked at last!" cried Edith, Dawnay, as she looked with blazing eyes at the man who claimed to be her husband's kin.

"I've got him!" came from the area door, which was now opened yet again. The voice, pleased and excited, was that of Eliot. "Here we are, Pointer, not too late, I hope. Here's Mr. Clark."

Sebastian spun round at the name. Lyall grinned wolfishly at his action. "The game's up at last, eh?" he snarled.

Eliot was showing a very little old man into the kitchen.

"This is Mr. Clark. He is, or was, the family solicitor of the Dawnays, who retired some twenty years ago, and this, Mr. Clark, is Chief Inspector Pointer of New Scotland Yard."

Pointer pulled out the only other chair in the room. It had no back, but Mr. Clark promptly perched himself on it, and sat staring across with his pale, red-rimmed eyes at the man staring back at him.

"He claims to be Sebastian Dawnay," Mrs. Dawnay said hotly, "Mr. Clark, you knew the Dawnay boys well as children. I've often heard my husband speak of you, and how good you were to them in their holidays. Do you recognise this man as Sebastian Dawnay?"

"Twenty-five years ago I saw a Sebastian Dawnay who had run away from his home. You expect me to identify this man as that boy? Twenty-five years ago! It can't be done, Mrs. Dawnay. I assured this young man as much, but he insisted on bringing me here from my home in Streatham—to perform the impossible." He turned to Eliot for the moment.

"But you can find out," Edith said imploringly. "Mr. Clark, you must help us! This man killed my husband—"

"That man killed Charles," Sebastian said, pointing to Lyall, "and would have killed you in that cupboard, if the chief inspector here hadn't been too quick for him. I confess I never thought of him being in there when I pushed you in—out of harm's way, I thought, if he should come back and there should be a rough-and-tumble."

Mr. Clark was listening and watching intently. He looked a shrewd old man, and very much all there as far as faculties went.

"I must get back home," he said now, rising and beginning to button up what looked like layers and layers of garments. "I told this young man I could be of no use. Now, sir, you will perhaps drive me back again." Again he spoke to and looked at Eliot.

"I was looking for you myself yesterday afternoon," Sebastian said. "I heard you had moved to Streatham."

"And moved again," nodded Mr. Clark.

"Ask him some questions, Mr. Clark," begged Edith Dawnay, "test him! Prove him to be an impostor!"

"I should be glad if you could see your way to help settle this matter," Pointer said courteously. He was watching the old solicitor intently.

"Well," said Mr. Clark, apparently after deep thought, "can you tell me—" and there followed three questions, each answered by Sebastian without a moment's trouble, though they seemed to take old Mr. Clark quite a long time to select from his memory. He nodded to each reply and looked again at Mrs. Dawnay, who stood biting her lip and quivering with disappointment and impatience—like Lyall. The only calm faces were those of Pointer, Eliot, Mallinson and, oddly enough, the man who claimed to be Sebastian Dawnay.

"Why, it isn't even locked," came the voice of Robina Miller in shocked tones. "I knew there was something on when you took so much trouble to slip out without being noticed, Sebastian. I had to pay the taximan an awful fare to follow, you twisted and turned so. But what's happening here?"

"Mr. Clark is trying to convince a lady who won't be convinced that I am Sebastian Dawnay," the man called by that name said gravely.

"Of course you're Sebastian!" came confidently and defiantly from Miss Miller.

"He's not Sebastian," Edith said firmly. "Robin, I'm sorry. I understand—and I'm sorry, but I can't keep silent. Nor would it be fair to you. This man murdered Charles, killed Major Hatton-Stroud and tried to murder Dr. Ozier."

"I'm damned if I did!" burst from the accused man. "Any of the lot! Charles was murdered by Lyall, because your husband intended to prevent his marrying Clare. Hatton-Stroud was the victim of a car accident, pure and simple. Ozier—well or ill, his health owes nothing to me. Chief inspector, you're a sportsman. What about Hatton-Stroud and Ozier?"

"We have no reason to think that Mr. Sebastian Dawnay—I call him by the only name by which I know him—so far, had anything to do with Major Hatton-Stroud's death. Dr. Ozier's illness is due to an accident of his own. And now I think," Pointer continued, "that it would be as well if you were to leave us for the moment, Mr. Lyall and Mr. Mallinson. Will you go back to Regency Avenue with Mrs. Dawnay, Miss Miller, and wait for us there? If we come to any decision in the matter, we will let you know. I will try to clear up the claims of this gentleman at once."

"But you can't tell—without help—who he is!" Edith Dawnay said despairingly.

"We have ways of testing evidence," Pointer said vaguely.

She hesitated, but Robina put an arm through hers. "I think we're better out of the way," said the younger woman. "It's stalemate apparently, as long as we're here. I came to help you, Sebastian, but I think you can be trusted to paddle your own canoe."

"Emphatically!" said Sebastian, in a tone of warm approval, "but I can't tell you, darling, how I appreciate—"

"I shall stay up to hear what happens—writing to Leslie," she said, and pulled Edith by the sleeve. "Come, Edie, we aren't wanted. Apparently the men want the floor to themselves to fight it out."

Mr. Clark chuckled like an amused crow, as the two women, one resolutely, one very haltingly, left the basement together.

"And now, gentlemen—" Pointer turned to Mallinson and Lyall.

"Come along in my car," said the solicitor, "we shall hear the truth later."

Lyall, who had altered strangely in looks since he had come into this dark little area, mumbled something, and followed him out. Mallinson drove away in silence. Then he stopped in a deserted street. "Suppose we get out and walk about a bit, and talk. Who really has that missing diary of Charles Dawnay's, I wonder!"

"I have it," Lyall said, "and it says you came at three o'clock, Mallinson."

"What?" burst incredulously from Mallinson. "Oh, I see! Of course, Dawnay entered the bogus appointment as with me. But we all know that."

"No, no!" said Lyall nastily, "it's after you came he made an entry. Says he had a talk with you and you left. When you came at four you were coming back to the summer-house."

"Preposterous!" said Mallinson scoffingly. "You're drunk, Lyall. Or Dawnay was."

"Now, I'm willing to let you have the diary—to destroy—for five hundred pounds," Lyall went on doggedly. "Notes, paid down at once. . . . Ah, would you!" He flung up the other's arm, and reached for a revolver in his own pocket.

In a second the two men were fighting on the pavement, now one, now the other, getting for a second the upper hand. Finally Lyall went down under a terrific blow from Mallinson, who had managed to get hold of the revolver.

A man came up at a run. He was a plain-clothes man who had been following them in another car. When they had jumped out he had lost them in the darkness of a crossing, and followed two other pedestrians who had resembled them sufficiently to be mistaken for them.

Mallinson was pretty well all-in, but he forced himself to speak clearly:

"Fetch the police. This man has just tried to murder me. Or better still, take me in a taxi to 2456 Tooting High Street . . . to Chief Inspector Point . . ." Mallinson felt his senses slipping. He had had a tremendous tussle.

"I know all about it, Mr. Mallinson," said the plain-clothes man, supporting him, "I'll take you there in a jiffy." He blew a whistle. "Must leave some one to look after the other one there," he explained. A policeman appeared. After exchanging a few words they helped the solicitor to the police car, and the plain-clothes man drove off with him for the house in Tooting.

There, the four men left alone had drawn closer as the sound of the last footstep died away.

Mr. Clark was fiddling with his gloves, Sebastian stood facing him, hands in pockets; Pointer was to one side, his quiet eyes looking first at one then at the other of the two men, while Eliot, his eyes round with interest, stood by the door. Eliot had always made his detective stand between the criminal and the door.

"First of all, I want you to think over your position, Mr. Dawnay. As I say, I don't know any other name to give you—" Pointer began.

"It's my own name!" came roughly from the man addressed.

"You're in an awkward position—to say the least of it," the chief inspector said, slowly. "If you cannot prove your identity, you will, obviously, be in a most dangerous position in regard to the murder of Mr. Charles Dawnay. Mr. Lyall has an alibi—you have none. Any motive on his part would be, as far as we yet know, inferential and may be non-existent. Yours would—in the case of an impersonation—leap to the eye. No jury would ask more."

"You think I'm your man, in short?" snapped Dawnay.

"I don't know," was the reply. " I only ask you, for your own sake, to explain yourself—if you can."

Looking at the other, Pointer saw that the man was feeling the strain. He was not often wrong in his reading of a face, and this one looked that of a man quite conscious of being in a most perilous position. Bold and daring the man was by nature, reckless possibly, though that was merely a guess from his swift movements and speech, but he was desperately frightened at the core of him, of that the chief inspector was certain. If an impostor, he was not prepared to have his bluff called. Or was it that he had all along needed no words to tell him that the accusation of impostor would only be the first step towards a capital charge. Pointer was sure, tough though the man looked, that he was sweating with fear.

As Sebastian kept silent, Pointer turned to the lawyer, who was biting his lip hard as he watched the scene.

"Mr. Clark, I wonder if a longer talk with this gentleman wouldn't help to clear up your mind as to his identity."

"No," said Mr. Clark, "I can't commit myself further than I have already, Impossible. Quite. Definitely. And now, if you'll excuse me, I think I must be getting home."

"Sorry, but I must ask for a little more help." Mr. Clark looked to him a very trustworthy man, conscientious and painstaking.

"I wonder if you would jot down for me a genealogical tree of the Dawnay family, beginning with the Sir John Dawnay from whom Mr. Charles Dawnay inherited his fortune. I shall get one on my return to the Yard, but I would like to see it now before I go there."

Mr. Clark hesitated, but took the sheet of paper held out to him and, getting out his fountain pen, drew a little tree. Pointer studied it. In front of Charles, as inheritors, came John Dawnay, marked as having died some fifteen years ago, and then a Lawrence Dawnay, marked as having died twelve years ago.

"Where did this John Dawnay die?" Pointer asked.

"At his home. Ennismore Gardens," Mr. Clark replied.

"And the next—this Mr. Lawrence Dawnay?"

"In Africa; in a fire at a Johannesburg hotel."

"Then are you Mr. Lawrence Dawnay?" Pointer asked instantly of the man called Sebastian.

The man's pupils dilated. The shot was utterly unexpected. But it was the solicitor's face that gave the show definitely away; that, and something in the silence of both men.

"You are," Pointer said promptly; "and I challenge you, or Mr. Clark here, to deny it?" Silence from both men.

"On the whole," Dawnay said at length, "I think it's my only card to play, Mr. Clark, eh? I mean, frankness."

Mr. Clark said nothing whatever. He gave the younger man a look that said he was retired and intended to stay so.

"I'll tell you exactly how matters stand," Dawnay said finally, very unwillingly, very reluctantly, "trusting to the Yard's reputed sense of honour to keep it secret. I wouldn't say as much as I am going to, but for the lucky chance of meeting old Clark. He recognises me all right, but doesn't quite know how to play the ball. You looked at the Dawnay family tree, Mr. Pointer, and you put your shot into the bull's eye. I am Lawrence Dawnay. This is the reason for my silence: I did quite well trading in general South African products, chiefly—unromantic reality—in eggs and poultry with a man named Richard Gant. The firm was Gant and Co. Gant sold me his share, but the firm's name remained, and I was more and more called Gant by people around—quite without my intending to change my name, be it understood, but quite willing to have a trade name. I met Charles and Edith out there on their honeymoon for an afternoon and liked them both immensely. Immensely. The next year her father, who was on the Baltic, was involved, quite without his fault, in the Copal Corner scandal and utterly ruined. Unfortunately, at first it looked as though his firm could be saved, and Charles, who admired and liked him tremendously, threw his own fortune, every penny, into the effort. Then came smash after smash, other creditors who had been considered safe were in their turn sucked under, and Mrs. Dawnay's father went bankrupt for about half a million, without a penny of assets. He died almost at once from pneumonia, caught by sitting up, oblivious to the cold, trying to get his papers into order. Then, within a month came the death of Sir John Dawnay and his huge legacy to his male next-of-kin. I got the news just at the time of the great Johannesburg fire which killed so many people. I was among the special constables enlisted to see that there was no looting and to help dig for bodies. I dug up several, and reported one more than was actually there, and gave that one the name of Lawrence Dawnay. Mind you, there was nothing quixotic about the matter. I didn't want to live in England—still don't want to. I was on to a splendid thing out there, which turned out even better than we hoped for. I didn't need the money and didn't want the life. It came as a godsend to Charles and Edith, and jolly good use he made of the money, and splendidly she filled the position down at Trenders. That's nearly ten years ago. But last year I rather wished I could see the old home again and link up with my people—or perhaps it was another meeting with my cousin, Sebastian Dawnay, which caused it, though he died of delirium tremens. A pal of his, a regular waster, had just gone off with all his money, when I chanced on him."

"Captain Dawson?" asked Pointer.

"Captain Dawson," assented Dawnay, "whom Mrs. Dawnay rather suspects me of being. He was up to his neck in the I.D.B. business and is, I think, in jail at the present time. But to return to Sebastian, I buried him way out on the veldt, and the idea came to me to use his name and go home for a holiday, meet my only relatives, Charles and Edie—I don't count Walter Lyall a relative, thank you—and see the old house. I never thought of any possible danger. Sebastian and I were alike as regards general build and colouring; I'm older, but that could be accounted for. I'm a Dawnay, and never thought of any doubt being cast on me, nor any reason why I should have to prove exactly who I was. I used Sebastian's passport, of course and with ease, came home, had a pleasant welcome from Charles and then found Edie growing rather a nuisance. For some reason or other she began to doubt me. I don't know what I did to rouse her suspicions, or whether it was something I didn't do. Anyway it only amused me to see her trying to test me. I led her on; pretended to forget a lot of things I knew all right. I didn't intend Edie to beat me at my own game, chief inspector. Once only I had a sort of shock, when it came up about Lawrence's death, and Charles said I was next to him in the line of old John's fortune unless Edie had a boy. But that was far off. Then came his murder the other day like a bolt from the blue, and I assure you, chief inspector, that, alibi or no alibi, Walter Lyall is your man. He's the murderer, and I'll tell you why," and Dawnay stressed the engagement which Charles would not permit, and the effort of Charles to turn a trick against Walter which would prevent the marriage to Clare. "He was only waiting for an opportunity, only looking round for a weapon—and I believe he had it under his hand, when Walter learnt of it and decided that he must, not live to use it".

Pointer asked many questions,, and noted down the replies.

The story stood up well under his questions, and they were clever ones.

Then Dawnay turned to the listening solicitor; "Mr. Clark, I've told the chief inspector who I am—do you mind telling him too? Confirmation of my own words. Do you recognise me?"

"Perfectly," came the reply.

"And my name is?"

"Lawrence Ogilvy Dawnay. Only son of Colonel John Dawnay of the Rifle Brigade and of his wife, Jessica, only daughter of—" but Dawnay assured him that would do.

"You have no doubts as to my identity?"

"None whatever," Clark said promptly, "nor of your folly in passing yourself off as Sebastian. I've heard your reasons, but consequences should be thought of first not last, and a more thoughtless, foolhardy idea than to come home as some one else."

"Yes, but I was dead, Mr. Clark, by my own act. So why not come to life by my own act too?"

"And are you going to inherit as Sebastian, and are you going to pay death duties quite needlessly a second time from what should have been your own estate all along?" demanded Mr. Clark. "And if you marry, will it be as Sebastian or Lawrence?"

Dawnay looked harassed. "I said I had no idea what I was bringing down on myself when I decided to run over as Sebastian and see Charles and the old place . . ." he said moodily. "I never meant to come a second time, and you bet I won't!"

"Not so easily avoided," was Mr. Clark's retort. "Look at the intricate position you've got into! And what about this accusation of murder? Is that supposed to be Lawrence's or Sebastian's doing?"

"The trouble is," Dawnay confessed, "that when I decided to be killed in that Johannesburg fire I did it thoroughly. I was using Gant as my business name more and more, and stuck to it from then on. I haven't a paper left to prove me really Lawrence. That's why I didn't own up to the chief inspector here immediately when the murder happened. I've no proof whatever of who I am. . . ."

Mr. Clark nodded his head as though to say that he expected as much.

"And by chance," went on Dawnay, "every soul who knows that the generally called Gant of the old days was really a Dawnay, is dead. I thought hard and I couldn't see how on earth I was going to prove who I was, chief inspector. Your finding Mr. Clark is a godsend."

"Eliot found him," Pointer said.

Eliot gave a gratified smile. He had found Mr. Clark when he was trying to discover which of Charles Dawnay's old friends might have had that all but accident the morning before in the City.

It was only when he had found that Clark had known the Dawnay boys so well, lived practically next door to them for many years, that it had occurred to him to ask the chief inspector over the telephone what he should do about him. Pointer had promptly told him to bring him to Tooting Main Road as soon as possible.

"Look here, Mr. Clark," Dawnay implored, and he did not often plead with any one for favours, "won't you help me? You must know ways and means to prove my identity? I don't want to claim the Dawnay money, but I can't let it go to Walter Lyall. It's my bounden duty to stop that murderer enjoying the money of his victim. If need be, I'll sacrifice myself and remain Sebastian Dawnay, or work my way back to civil life as Lawrence, rather than that."

"A very much easier thing to say than to do," was the comforting reply; "but we may be able to get him hung."

"I don't want him hung," Sebastian went on soberly. "Him rather than me, naturally, as I know he's the murderer, but after all, he is my kin. Look here, chief inspector, what was the real reason for this little party he gave? Why are we all collected down here? Has he got the diary, or has Mrs. Dawnay?"

"Why were you so keen on having that diary, Mr. Dawnay?" Pointer asked, though he knew the reply.

"Because, according to Mrs. Dawnay, Charles had jotted down his doubts of me, and some questions he intended to ask me, which I am certain I couldn't have answered. Sebastian and I never saw much of each other at the best of times. With nothing to prove my story, with such a motive to have murdered Charles—a double motive. . . . God, of course, I want that diary in my own safe keeping!"

Mr. Clark's eye said that Sebastian was talking far too much, as the solicitor got shakily to his feet and said he must be getting back to his home. It wasn't by keeping late hours and going in for excitement that he had lived to be eighty-five.

Dawnay, who had thought him long dead, dutifully saw him safely into a taxi. Then he returned hot-foot. "You haven't told me yet, chief inspector, what the idea of this meeting down here really is. You seem to have it all well in hand. I take it that it's of your contriving? "

There was a knock on the area door. The plainclothes man helped Mallinson into the room, a very battered and tattered Mallinson, with one black and one green eye.

CHAPTER SEVENTEEN

"CHIEF INSPECTOR," Mallinson began, trying to find where his collar was with one swollen hand, "I'm afraid I've stunned Mr. Lyall. I had to, in self-defence. He attacked me without the slightest provocation . . . murderously. . . . I suppose because this evening's party did not go according to his plan."

Pointer was handed a note by the plain-clothes man explaining how he had found Lyall and Mallinson after losing them.

"And what was that?" broke in Dawnay. "Where is he, by the way?"

"I'm afraid he's being attended to by the local police," Mallinson said in a tone of apology. "I didn't hit him half hard enough, as a matter of fact, for he intended you to be arrested for Mrs. Dawnay's murder, Mr. Dawnay."

"What?" came from Dawnay and Eliot simultaneously. Pointer did not look surprised. He had a very clear idea of what this meeting had been meant to be and do. But at that moment he was called to the telephone in the chemist's shop overhead. He had arranged with them to be called if necessary. Mr. Bonar had been found, and had at once handed over what he did not know that he had — Charles Dawnay's diary. The man had not yet gone through the contents of the box. Pointer was given full details—in code—then he went downstairs again.

Mallinson asked for a glass of water and took a deep drink, then went on, his voice husky, as his throat had been badly squeezed.

"Of course! That was the idea of getting you two here with the bait of the diary which Lyall claimed to have found. He himself had got that, of course, and destroyed it at once."

"But about Mrs. Dawnay and me," pressed Dawnay.

"He expected you to kill her for it, I think," was Mallinson's startling statement.

"Oh, come now!" said Eliot, but Dawnay looked speculative, and the chief inspector nodded.

"You think so too?" queried Eliot, impressed.

"I do," was the reply. "But let Mr. Mallinson continue. He may know more of the details."

But Mallinson had only his profound conviction of what Lyall meant to do. He expanded, however, his dreadful idea, which was also the theory of the chief inspector, that Lyall, thinking Sebastian Dawnay capable of anything, knowing, once he had learnt that Sebastian was probably an impostor, how all-important the diary would be to him, had banked on Mrs. Dawnay's pluck, and her refusal to let her husband's kinsman get hold of the diary. Had she had it, she would certainly have let herself be killed rather than give it up to the man whom she believed had murdered her husband.

"I am certain he would then have given you in charge for murdering her and Charles Dawnay," went on Mallinson. "That was why I came along and, though I thought it better not to be officially on the scene, I stood outside close to the window to come on in at the first cry from her."

"Luckily the chief inspector didn't wait for that much even," Dawnay said warmly. "Was that why you were at the cupboard so quickly when I shoved her into that viper's arms? My metaphor is mixed—so are my brains just now."

Pointer gave an assenting nod.

"Would he have strangled her if you hadn't jumped to it so instantly?" Dawnay asked in a tone of sudden horror. And again Pointer nodded.

"Good God!" came from Eliot, who pressed for details.

Dawnay gave them. "I wanted that diary—badly," he added "I wanted her out of the way if Lyall should dash back and fight me for it. I shoved her into his arms not knowing he was in the cupboard, and he gripped her throat on the instant. Claimed he didn't want her to scream the house down when the chief inspector hauled her out. By God, what an escape? He would have sworn afterwards that I did it. And in truth I should have been almost as much her murderer as he." Dawnay was quite white under his tan. "And, of course, I'd have been living, and she'd have been dead."

"Who killed Charles Dawnay? He did, I suppose?" Mallinson asked, taking another gulp of water.

"But when?" Pointer cut in. "When? That's the problem."

"He had a talk with Dawnay at half-past two," said Mallinson, wishing the room would settle down to stability again.

"And he meant to murder Mrs. Dawnay and have me hung for the double crime," Dawnay said meditatively. "Well, I won't promise what will happen when we meet again—in the very near future!"

"Yes," Pointer said slowly, "I think he thought that Mrs. Dawnay was best out of the way in case her baby should be a boy. And as you, he believed, had murdered Mr. Charles Dawnay, he thought that murder probably came easy to you. Nearly as easy as it did to himself, apparently."

"Thought I murdered Charles!" repeated Dawnay. "But how could he?"

"When he murdered him himself," Eliot reminded the chief inspector, with a half laugh. "We're none of us quite ourselves after this upset, I take it," he said excusingly.

Pointer was always himself, at any hour of the day or night, under any circumstances, physical or mental.

"No, Mr. Lyall didn't murder Mr. Charles Dawnay," he now said quietly, "Mr. Mallinson did that. Just as he has now murdered, or at least killed, Mr. Lyall under the plea of self-protection. Henry Mallinson, I arrest you on the double charge of—" and he walked over to the man who, white-faced, had risen, giddily to his feet.

"What—what—it's a lie! Lyall dead? I hit him in self-defence—look at my own condition. He attacked me like a wolf. And as to Dawnay, he murdered him when he came at half-past two, I tell you. He got Clare Dawnay to swear she was with him from two on, but she wasn't! He didn't join her till just before three!"

"And how do you know that? Because, you yourself telephoned to Mr. Dawnay to give you an appointment at three; you came then, saw him in the summer-house, heard about his talk with Mr. Lyall, learnt from him facts which would not permit your proceeding unmolested with the sale of the concessions on which you were about to buy an option, for which you had already borrowed heavily —and, I think, sold some client's securities. The all-important sale was for the next day. Lest that should fall through, you killed Mr. Dawnay, and walked out of the gates, carefully posting a letter which he had given to you, which contained his diary by mistake instead of the one which he thought that he was returning—the discovery of the game which his cousin Lyall was playing had upset him thoroughly. You had gloves on when you brought that cudgel down on his head, but after planting it in the flowerr-bed you took them off for fear of leaving earth or green smears on the envelope. It has your fingerprints on it in unusually good condition, Mr. Mallinson, and the post was collected at three-thirty from that box. The postmark alone proved when you came!"

"Also you were really the inciter in this project of Lyall's which went astray. You told him of this address, you suggested to Mrs. Dawnay that she should try to enrage Mr. Dawnay here. As to the murder of Mr. Lyall, I think he tried to frighten you, I think you believed he really had the missing diary—you probably now have in your pocket the book he was carrying, the book placed by us in that tin box. . . . We have the real one, Mr. Charles Dawnay's missing diary, in which he records briefly his talk with you at three o'clock, entered probably after he had chatted about the accident in the morning, telling you details such as retrieving the man's umbrella and hat, which Mr. Lyall did not know. I think he asked you to drop the envelope in the pillar-box when you left, and you thought it best to carry out this request. You did not notice the one discarded envelope which he had used as a spill to light his pipe."

"He didn't make any entry—I mean in the street—" came from Mallinson the last added as though in correction of the former sentence.

"He probably did so when he slipped away from the summer-house for a moment—perhaps when he fetched the papers found in one of the drawers of the writing table in the summer-house, which have to do with Bolivian floods and tides," was the reply—a mere guess on the chief inspector's part.

Something showed in Mallinson's eyes for a second. He had quite forgotten that momentary absence of his host to fetch some more papers with which to prove his point—that the concessions were in reality worthless because of a certain tide in the river which would seep through into the workings and practically undo in a few weeks all the efforts to shore up which had taken months of labour. So that was when Charles Dawnay had entered a note about his visit. . . . Damn Charles Dawnay anyway . . . his head was going round and round.

He was taken away after that in a somewhat belated silence, and the pocket-diary bought by Pointer was found on him. He had taken it from Lyall in the fight.

"And you say Walter Lyall is really and truly dead?" Dawnay asked. He did not pretend to any sorrow at the idea.

"Hit on the head by the same kind of a blow that killed his cousin," Pointer said—"a terrific blow. Mallinson wanted to get rid of him . . . he must have either bluffed too near the truth, or guessed that Mallinson had after all been the man who telephoned, that he really had put his appointment at three, and came—the first time—on the hour."

Pointer did not know it then, but later on, the prosecution had an unexpected ally in Gipsy Joe, who had been watching the house, meditating an entry to recover his cudgel. He had seen Mallinson arrive just before three and leave within a quarter of an hour, post something in the pillar-box, and hurry away in his car. Gipsy Joe had not been there when Mallinson came the second time— the time which he claimed as his first arrival, but there was no doubt about the verdict once those fingerprints on the envelope containing the missing diary had been found.

The cipher provided the one bright spot of the grim trial. Experts had struggled hard with it, some believing themselves to be near success. Mr. Bonar explained that he was interested in pickling eggs, and that the figures represented the number of eggs pickled by him, the marks above, or beneath, the brackets round, or square, signifying what particular form of preservative he had used, as he was anxious to test all the different kinds on the market. He was making quite a good thing out of his "Home Preserved Eggs" and was anxious to obtain all possible tests.

Who the so-called Sebastian Dawnay really was did not come out in public, greatly though it would have interested the reporters. Mallinson himself had been told the true facts at once, so as to prevent his putting Dawnay forward as the murderer. Mallinson's counsel tried to make a case for his client out of Colonel Richards' efforts to keep him away from the house, but as that odd incident only rested on Mallinson's own word, and as the gallant colonel absolutely denied having been anywhere near the house in question, the defence found that the jury refused to take the incident as real, greatly to Mallinson's indignation.

"Did you suspect Mr. Dawnay of being an impostor?" Robina Miller asked Pointer, when she learnt the real name of the man to whom she was engaged.

"If I tell you, will you tell me—" Pointer paused.

"Who Leslie is," threw in Dawnay, who was in the room. "I tell Robin she ought to be our best bridesmaid."

Pointer, for once, had no clue to the speech. "If I tell you, will you in your turn tell me just what the trouble was between you and Mrs. Dawnay?" he asked Miss Miller.

Pointer was very curious to know if his private guess was near the truth. It was.

"Why don't you ask her yourself, chief inspector? Since you saved her from Walter, she would do anything for you. For the poor darling realised, she says, when Walter's hand closed around her throat, that he meant murder and not merely to stifle any shrieks of hers. But before you look her up at Cromer, tell me whether you suspected Sebastian of being Captain something-or-other, or not."

"I thought he was certainly a Dawnay," Pointer replied. "I went down to the family portrait gallery, and he seemed to me to be quite unmistakably of that breed. Nor had I a suspicion, until I saw the way she took Major Hatton-Stroud's death, of what was at the back of Mrs. Dawnay's attitude to him."

"And when the frightfully cautious Mr. Clark wouldn't vouch for him?" she asked with a smile.

"But he didn't protest at his claim to be a Dawnay," Pointer said, "as I would have expected him to do had Mr. Dawnay been an impostor. And he was very careful to think over the questions he asked him before putting them, yet each of the three was of a kind that any member of the family could have been expected to know, whether Sebastian or not—but not an outsider."

"That was why you wanted to see the family tree and spotted who he was so instantly?"

Pointer said that that was why. He went on to say that the police had just got the man whose car had run into Major Hatton-Stroud's and caused that most inopportune death—one which had added immeasurably to the suspicions of Sebastian in Mrs. Dawnay's mind.

At Cromer, Pointer found Mrs. Dawnay, white and fragile looking, with her children. She considered it as part of her penance to tell the chief inspector what he had finally guessed, the reason for her, having stood behind the curtains in her own dining-room the last time that she ever saw her husband.

Incidentally, Mrs. Dawnay's baby was a son, and so Lawrence Dawnay returned to South Africa, there took the name of Gant, and as Gant married Robina Miller, who had always protested that she knew that he was Sebastian Dawnay, when, as a matter of fact, she had not been at all as sure as she claimed to be.

Mrs. Dawnay would have preferred not to have her son inherit the fortune which really was Lawrence Dawnay's, but that man's urgent adjurations, and old Mr. Clark's reiterations as to the years of death-duty squabbles that would ensue, finally made her give way.

"When did you first suspect the real criminal?" Major Pelham, the Assistant Commissioner, once asked Pointer, long after the trial and the execution were over.

"It was always a possibility, sir, when we could find no one who seemed to fit that arrival at three o'clock, for Mallinson had a peculiar voice. It seemed rather odd that so acute a man as Mr. Charles Dawnay was considered to be should not have noticed the difference of voice so soon after he had been talking to Mr. Mallinson, and talking in the street too, when one has rather to force one's voice— as Mallinson did over the telephone, I noticed. But it was when I found that he had told me—as having been mentioned by Mr. Charles Dawnay in that first encounter—of an incident which had taken place after their morning meeting, that I wondered whether he might not have heard of it from Mr. Dawnay later on in the day. According to Mallinson, there was no such second meeting, but he mentioned a few points which were unknown to Lyall, the man from whom he professed to have learnt of this incident. After that, the only question seemed to be to find sufficient proof. We know that some one had come—the murderer—and had probably been asked by Mr. Dawnay to post a diary in an envelope—as he himself had a sore foot and was wearing carpet slippers."

"Mallinson's infatuation for Mrs. Dawnay was one of the odd little gleams in that affair," mused Major Pelham aloud. He caught the chief inspector's eye.

"You don't think it was genuine?"

"I do not, sir. I think he only wanted an excuse for going a great deal to the house, and so keeping in touch with the case. Personally, I don't believe he had ever met her before. Mrs. Dawnay is positive that she had never seen him, let alone talked to him, until he showed up at Regency Avenue."

"Ah, well, that certainly makes it much less odd—and much more in keeping with the man's utterly heartless character," Pelham said, laying down his cigar.

THE END

Other Resurrected Press Books in *The Chief Inspector Pointer Mystery* Series

Murder at Bridge

When an afternoon bridge party attended by some of Hamilton's leading citizens ends with the hostess being murdered in her boudoir, Special Investigator Dundee of the District Attorney's office is called in. But one of the attendees is guilty? There are plenty of suspects: the victim's former lover, her current suitor, the retired judge who is being blackmailed, the victim's maid who had been horribly disfigured accidentally by the murdered woman, or any of the women who's husbands had flirted with the victim. Or was she murdered by an outsider whose motive had nothing to do with the town of Hamilton. Find the answer in... **Murder at Bridge**

One Drop of Blood

When Dr. Koenig, head of Mayfield Sanitarium is murdered, the District Attorney's Special Investigator, "Bonnie" Dundee must go undercover to find the killer. Were any of the inmates of the asylum insane enough to have committed the crime? Or, was it one of the staff, motivated by jealousy? And what was is the secret in the murdered man's past. Find the answer in... **One Drop of Blood**

- The Problem of Cell 13 by Jacques Futrelle
- The Conundrum of the Golf Links by Percy James Brebner
- The Silkworms of Florence by Clifford Ashdown
- The Gateway of the Monster by William Hope Hodgson
- The Affair at the Semiramis Hotel by A. E. W. Mason
- The Affair of the Avalanche Bicycle & Tyre Co., LTD by Arthur Morrison

RESURRECTED PRESS CLASSIC MYSTERY CATALOGUE

Journeys into Mystery
Travel and Mystery in a More Elegant Time

The Edwardian Detectives
Literary Sleuths of the Edwardian Era

Gems of Mystery
Lost Jewels from a More Elegant Age

E. C. Bentley
Trent's Last Case: The Woman in Black

Ernest Bramah
Max Carrados Resurrected:
The Detective Stories of Max Carrados

Agatha Christie
The Secret Adversary
The Mysterious Affair at Styles

Octavus Roy Cohen
Midnight

Freeman Wills Croft
The Ponson Case
The Pit Prop Syndicate

J. S. Fletcher
The Herapath Property
The Rayner-Slade Amalgamation
The Chestermarke Instinct
The Paradise Mystery
Dead Men's Money

Fergus Hume
The Mystery of a Hansom Cab
The Green Mummy
The Silent House
The Secret Passage

Edgar Jepson
The Loudwater Mystery

A. E. W. Mason
At the Villa Rose

A. A. Milne
The Red House Mystery
Baroness Emma Orczy
The Old Man in the Corner

Edgar Allan Poe
The Detective Stories of Edgar Allan Poe

Arthur J. Rees
The Hampstead Mystery
The Shrieking Pit
The Hand In The Dark
The Moon Rock
The Mystery of the Downs

Mary Roberts Rinehart
Sight Unseen and The Confession

Dorothy L. Sayers
Whose Body?

Sir William Magnay
The Hunt Ball Mystery

Mabel and Paul Thorne
The Sheridan Road Mystery

Louis Tracy
The Strange Case of Mortimer Fenley
The Albert Gate Mystery
The Bartlett Mystery
The Postmaster's Daughter
The House of Peril
The Sandling Case: What Would You Have Done?
Charles Edmonds Walk
The Paternoster Ruby

John R. Watson
The Mystery of the Downs
The Hampstead Mystery

Edgar Wallace
The Daffodil Mystery
The Crimson Circle

Carolyn Wells
Vicky Van
The Man Who Fell Through the Earth
In the Onyx Lobby
Raspberry Jam
The Clue
The Room with the Tassels
The Vanishing of Betty Varian
The Mystery Girl
The White Alley
The Curved Blades
Anybody but Anne
The Bride of a Moment
Faulkner's Folly
The Diamond Pin
The Gold Bag
The Mystery of the Sycamore
The Come Backy

Raoul Whitfield
Death in a Bowl

And much more!
Visit ResurrectedPress.com
for our complete catalogue

About Resurrected Press

A division of Intrepid Ink, LLC, Resurrected Press is dedicated to bringing high quality, vintage books back into publication. See our entire catalogue and find out more at www.ResurrectedPress.com.

About Intrepid Ink, LLC

Intrepid Ink, LLC provides full publishing services to authors of fiction and non-fiction books, eBooks and websites. From editing to formatting, from publishing to marketing, Intrepid Ink gets your creative works into the hands of the people who want to read them. Find out more at www.IntrepidInk.com.